D1795729

FIXATION

FIXATION IS THE BRAND NEW
PSYCHOLOGICAL THRILLER FROM
L. POWELL, THE CREATOR OF THE
PERFECT SERIES...

Books by L. Powell

The Perfect Series
Perfect Stranger
Perfect Memories
Perfect Disaster
Perfect Beginnings

Stand-alone novels
Fixation

THEY SAY, 'KEEP YOUR FRIENDS CLOSE AND YOUR ENEMIES CLOSER...' BUT SOMETIMES THE ENEMY CAN BE DANGEROUS.....

Chapter One.

Sitting by myself, looking out of the café window, I wonder where I went wrong in life. I may only be twenty-eight, but I can honestly say that my life has not panned out the way I was expecting. Being an only child, I never had a sibling to grow up with. I never had someone who would always look out for me and be there for me when I needed them. You would think that I would have acquired some close friends during my years of school and college, but sadly that was not the case. I never fitted in anywhere. I was always classed as the odd one out. I guess it could have been down to the fact that I have always been shy, but deep down I just use that as an excuse. I have no idea why people don't take to me. Even my parents aren't bothered about me. I get the odd text message from my mum, but nothing more than that. Her drinking habit may have something to do with that though.

As a teen, I had to deal with her drunken outbursts which often resulted in me having to clean up her vomit and get her changed out of her piss-soaked clothes. My dad left my mum and I when I was thirteen years old. So, not only did I have to deal with the struggle of trying to fit in at school, but I also had to deal with the fallout from my dad leaving. There was no time for me to grieve as my mum's drinking got worse by the day. She has never recovered from her broken heart. My dad was her world, and I reminded her of him far too much after his departure. She took her anger out on me. I was all that she had left. Unfortunately, her behaviour pushed me away.

Our contact became less and less once I moved out and got my own place. For the first time in years, I had my own breathing space.

To have my own place was heaven for the first few weeks. I no longer had to deal with my mum's outbursts. I no longer had to feel like her servant, cleaning up her messes. I could just be 'me.' I was able to afford to live on my own after landing a manager's job at the local newspaper. I wasn't a journalist or anything like that, I had no interest in scoping out stories for people to feast upon. Being shy, I felt more comfortable being in an office, but I needed a job that would pay my expenses and becoming the office manager helped me to do that. Yes, I was shy, but I wanted to get away from my mum more, so I made myself delegate. I made myself tell people what to do. I had managed to come out of college with a decent grade in management which is what essentially got me the job in the first place. I think that, if it had been down to personality alone, then I may have been screwed. Lucky for me, the other applicants had clearly not been as qualified as I was.

My days consisted of work and going back to my little home. I didn't go out for drinks with work colleagues. No one asked me, and I never asked to go. I would listen to them discuss their post-work drinking plans, but I would never involve myself. Of course I would feel a slight pang of jealousy, but I would push it away. I didn't expect anything different. I just kept my head down, collected my pay check at the end of the month, and I did the same thing day in and day out. Weekends could be boring, but at least I was saving some money by not going out and pissing it all up against the wall. The only thing I allowed myself was a Saturday morning coffee at a café in town. That is what I am doing now. Sipping a creamy latte whilst sitting by the window and watching strangers go about their day.

I stay in the café for about an hour before I decide to walk back home. I leave the money on the table for my drink and I stand up, putting my coat on and wrapping it tightly around me. Winter is starting to set in, and the cold November wind is biting as I step out into the fresh air. I shiver slightly from the change in temperature and then I turn to walk in the direction of my house. I focus my eyes on the pavement in front of me, and I am lost in my own thoughts, which is why I don't notice the person walking towards me until I bump right into them. As I collide with a hard chest, I let out a yelp as I ricochet backwards which causes me to stumble and lose my footing. I feel a hand wrap around my arm to stop me from falling on my ass. My hair starts to whip wildly round my face from the force of the wind, distorting my view of the person who is currently wrapping their other arm around my waist to steady me.

"Are you okay?" A deep voice asks me. A voice that has my heart accelerating slightly. I don't fail to notice that the guy still has his arm around my waist, even though I am no longer at risk of falling, and I suddenly feel self-conscious that he is touching me. No guy has ever touched me. No guy has ever been near me.

"Uh……" I don't know what to say. I feel like an idiot as I try to calm my racing thoughts. I move my hand to my face, and I brush the hair out of my eyes. As I attempt to straighten myself out, I finally get my first proper glimpse of the man in question. The man who is still holding me. His eyes capture me first. Striking emerald iris's that seem to sparkle. Eyes that I could lose myself in. Eyes that are making me feel butterflies in my stomach. Something that I haven't experienced before. I force myself to look elsewhere as I take in the rest of him. He has light brown hair that has a slight wave to it, a strong jaw line and a masculine frame. His suit screams that he is a business man, along with the briefcase that I can now see has been placed on the pavement, by the side of him. I have no idea when he placed it there due to my dazed reaction.

"Miss?" His voice alerts me, breaking my perusal of him.

"Sorry," I reply a little breathlessly. I'm hoping that he just puts my lack of breath down to the fact that I have bumped into him, rather than the fact that my heart is beating ten to the dozen at how handsome he is. "I'm fine. I didn't mean to walk into you."

"No, it was my fault," he says as he removes his hand from my waist and my arm, clearly being convinced that I am now okay to be left unsupported. Little does he know that I am battling with myself not to melt into a gooey puddle due to his good looks. "I didn't see you as I was too busy looking at my phone. Guess I should take more notice of where I am going huh?" He smiles, and I feel myself blush. His smile is dazzling.

"Honestly, it was my fault too."

"Let me buy you a cup of coffee as my way of saying sorry." I physically recoil from his words. Not because I don't want to, but because this is new territory. *He wants to buy me a drink? He doesn't want to get away from me as quickly as possible?* I can feel my eyebrows knit together in confusion, and his smile drops slightly. "It's okay if you don't want to of course." *Do I want to? Should I go? Why is this decision so shocking to me? Why can't I just be normal? This must happen all the time to other people, so why should it be any different now that it is happening to me? It's just coffee. It's not a ridiculous request. Come on Kayleigh, grab a slice of 'normal' and go for a drink with the guy.* Before I can stop myself, I utter the one word that could change the course that my life has been following for years.

"Okay."

Chapter Two.
Three Years Later.
May 11th 2017.

"Will you marry me?" The words that I have longed to hear for so long are like music to my ears. I am sat in a restaurant, with Ben knelt on one knee before me. I feel tears spring to my eyes as all of my dreams are coming true. Ben looks at me, his green eyes captivating me just as they did on the first day that I met him three years ago. I am so thankful that I wasn't looking where I was going on that fateful day where I met the love of my life. I don't keep him waiting as I swallow past the lump in my throat and I give him the answer that is going to mark this as the happiest day of my life.

"Yes." He smiles as he takes the ring out of the box that he is holding. Placing the box on the table beside us, he then takes my hand and pushes the delicate silver band onto my finger. The ring is perfect. Nothing too fancy, but definitely a ring that I would have chosen myself. Three tiny diamonds are embedded into the silver. I watch as he places a kiss on my hand and then moves towards me, taking me in his arms and wrapping his hands around my waist. I move forward on my seat as much as possible and hold him close to me. I inhale his masculine scent and close my eyes. I never thought that I could be this happy. I never thought that I could love someone so much, and have that love returned. Ben has filled the void in my life that has been there for as long as I can remember. I was destined to meet him. He has made me see that life can be good.

"I love you," he whispers in my ear, causing goose-bumps to trail over my body.

"I love you too," I reply as I allow a few tears to slip down my cheeks. Ben pulls away slightly and places a light kiss on my lips. With our love growing with each day that passes, I honestly don't think that things could get any better. When our kiss ends, Ben gets up off of the floor and takes his seat opposite me. I allow my eyes to look around the room and I notice a few people looking our way, and each one of them has a smile on their face. I feel elation consume me as I look back to the ring on my finger.

"Surprised?" Ben asks me, drawing my attention back to him.

"Just a bit."

"Surely you had a bit of an inkling that I was going to propose?"

"Not at all." Even though I have been with Ben for three years, I never allow myself to hope beyond the here and now. My previous years taught me to be somewhat guarded, and to never expect things to go the way that you want. "I can't believe it."

"Why not?"

"You know my past Ben and you know what I have been through." I look down feeling ashamed about my life before him.

"Hey," he says softly, reaching across the table and placing his hand on top of mine. "You have no reason to doubt anymore Kayleigh. Your past has no place in our future." I love that he knows just what to say to stop my mind from going back to the dark place that it once resided.

"I know," I whisper. "It's just, it's hard for me to completely let my guard down." He already knows this, and he has been so patient with me over the years. Sometimes I wonder why he puts up with me.

"It's time to let it down. I'm not going anywhere." I can see that he means what he says, and I hate that there is still a part of me that doubts him. It's only a very small part, but it's still there.

"I'll try."

"Good. Now, how about we order a bottle of champagne to celebrate?" His grin is infectious, and I allow myself to revel in my moment of happiness.

"That sounds perfect." Ben calls one of the waiters over and places the order. I find myself looking back to my engagement ring every few seconds just to check that I haven't dreamt the last few moments. *I'm engaged. Me.* I am no longer the odd one out. I am just a normal woman, celebrating a momentous occasion with the one person who has restored me. I was broken when I met Ben, a shadow of the person that I am today. Letting the last part of my doubt go is my final hurdle. *I can do this. I trust him, and I trust that he will always be by my side.* No one can break us, and no one can destroy our life together. I can finally allow myself to picture the future. A future where I will be Mrs Benjamin Connors.

The waiter returns with the champagne and pours each of us a glass, leaving the bottle in a cooler by the side of the table. Ben takes his glass at the same time that I take mine.

"To us," he says, raising his glass in the air. I clink my glass against his as I repeat the words that he just spoke.

"To us." The bubbles from the champagne almost tickle my tongue before the cool liquid slides down my throat.

"Do you like the ring?" Ben asks me when he has finished drinking. I place my glass back on the table and reach across for his hand. I link my fingers with his as I hold my left hand out with the ring on for us both to look at.

"I love it."

"Thank goodness for that. I was a bit worried that I made a mistake by not getting one with a bigger diamond."

"No way, this is exactly what I would have chosen."

"Phew. It just shows that Monica was right."

"Monica?"

"I showed her the two rings that I had narrowed it down to, and she told me that less was more."

"Oh right." I feel my happiness leave me at the mention of another woman's name. A woman that I am sure I haven't heard him mention before. "And how would this Monica person have known which one I would have preferred?" I can hear the bite to my tone, but I can't mask it. I feel like I have been sucker-punched. A few seconds ago I was floating on cloud nine, and now I am feeling floored.

"She wouldn't know. I just asked her opinion on which one was best." I don't answer him. I feel cold and I shiver slightly. "Are you okay?" He asks me, genuinely not understanding why my mood has changed significantly.

"Yeah." I pick up my champagne glass and down the remainder.

"Kayleigh, what's wrong?" I refill my own glass and take a few more sips as he waits for me to answer. Can he seriously not figure it out for himself?

"I just, I thought that you had chosen the ring by yourself, not got some other woman to do it for you. A woman that I don't even know might I add." I fold my arms across my chest feeling the need to create a barrier of some description.

"Oh Kayleigh," he says whilst chuckling. My eyes widen at his relaxed response. *He's laughing about it? I'm sat here seething, and he just finds it funny?* "Babe, Monica is Jerry's wife. She happened to be in the office when I was telling Jerry that I was planning to propose and that is how I asked for her opinion on the ring." I feel myself shrink in the chair at his answer. Jerry is Ben's boss. Of course he would show the boss's wife the rings if she asked. The anger melts away as quickly as it came.

"Oh god, I'm sorry. I just….." My voice trails off as I realise how ridiculous I have been.

"It's okay. I guess I could have worded it better."

"No don't apologise, I shouldn't think the worst. I need to stop thinking that you are going to leave me."

"Yes you should. I have told you that I'm not going anywhere, and I mean it. I love you, and I want to spend the rest of my life with you." His words break the defences that I had up just moments ago. This just reiterates why I need to let the doubts go. Ben loves me. I'm not going to ruin this. I won't let myself push away the one person that has done nothing but be there for me.

"Can we just forget the last few moments?" I say, my cheeks flushing with embarrassment.

"Sure." I smile at him and allow myself to relax. Ben is mine, and I would fight anyone who wanted to take him away from me. I will quieten the voice in my head that continues to try to sabotage my happiness. The voice that has been with me since I was little. The voice that won't let me be happy. The voice that continues to tell me that I am not good enough……

Chapter Three.

A few days have passed since Ben's proposal, and I find myself standing outside my mum's front door. I don't owe her anything, and I haven't spoken to her for about a year, but I feel the need to tell her about the next chapter in my life. I guess I am looking for her approval, even though she has never met Ben and even though she has never cared what route my life has taken. A small part of me still hopes for the mum that she used to be, before the alcohol took over her personality. I still crave acceptance, and I am hoping that by acquiring some acceptance that I will be able to quiet the nagging voice in my head that continues to try to ruin my happiness. I promised myself that I would do everything that I could to let go of all of the pain that I have endured. I promised that I wouldn't let the voice come between Ben and I. Ben means so much to me, and he has helped me in ways that I never thought that he could have. My confidence has grown, I feel better about myself in some ways, and he has made me try new things. I even speak to people that I don't really know now, even if it is only a few words, I make myself talk. I don't always shy away into the background now. And I need to apply that confidence when I confront my mum. She could break my progress, but she could also heal me completely. If I don't do this then I am scared that the voice will take over my life again, and I really don't want that to happen.

I raise my hand and knock on her front door three times before I drop my hand and wait. The waiting seems to take forever, and I am about to knock again, when I hear someone stumbling behind the front door. I turn my head to the side so that I can listen better. All I can make out is the sound of my mum cursing whilst she sounds like she is banging into everything that she possibly can. I can only assume that she is drunk. It's awful that that is the first thought that comes into my head. Most kids would be concerned that their parents were having some trouble moving something or falling over something. In my case I have no concern. This is the norm. I start to tap my foot on the floor as I continue to wait. A part of me wants to give up and retreat but I won't let myself. I repeat, 'this might quiet the voice. Don't walk away. Wait and see,' over and over again. I need to think about the bigger picture. The bigger picture that would allow me to be doubt free and completely in control of my thoughts. I take deep breaths to calm myself. As I wait, I close my eyes and think of Ben. About how he loves me and how he only wants the best for me. I'm becoming a better person for him. It scares me that he might get fed up and leave me one day, but he keeps assuring me that he won't, and I have to trust his words.

Eventually, I hear the door being unlocked. I open my eyes and brace myself for the state that my mum could be in. Who am I trying to kid, of course she will be in a state. She always is. As the door starts to open, I hold my breath, the musty smell hitting my nostrils through the gap in the door. My eyes take in the grime that I can see over the floor and the walls. Yellow stains on the threadbare carpet and nicotine stains covering the outdated wallpaper. As my eyes follow the door opening, nothing could have prepared me for the sight of my mum. I gasp at her sickly thin frame. Her eyes widen when she finally focuses them on me and recognition triggers.

"Kayleigh?" Her weak voice asks me. I want to cry for her. I want to stand here and cry for the mess that my mum has made of herself. I nod my head, afraid that if I talk then I won't be able to keep the hurt out of my voice. I take in her limp, thin hair which once cascaded in curls down her back. I take in her clothes which are clearly years old judging by the out-dated pattern of her jumper. The leggings that cover her skinny legs are too baggy, and there are various holes in them which look like cigarette burns. There are no shoes on her feet, just some dirty socks which I am sure are contributing to the atrocious smells wafting their way outside. What really makes me sad though are her eyes. Her once vibrant blue eyes appear to be dull and lifeless. Her hope has left her. Her sparkle a distant memory. I don't want to end up like this. I don't want to follow in the footsteps of my mum.

"Can I come in?" I ask, making myself talk. I need to get this over and done with. There is no helping her, but I can help myself and that is what I need to focus on.

"Sure." She waves me in and I take a step inside. My mum closes the front door and I wait, trying not to let myself touch anything. I have never seen so much dirt in one place. It makes me shiver in revulsion. "Follow me, we can sit in the lounge." I do as she asks, but I don't think that I will be sitting on anything in the lounge if it is in the same state as the hall way. My nose screws up, the smells getting stronger as we walk deeper into the house. The lounge door is on the right and when I walk in I have to stop myself from speaking. This room is in a worse state than the hall way. I come to a stop in the doorway and take in the two sofas that have no covering left on them. They are just pieces of foam, with various chunks taken out of them. The carpet has so many stains on it that I am unable to see what colour it was to begin with. There is no television, no ornaments and no pictures anywhere. There is nothing personal in this room whatsoever. My mum takes a seat on the sofa to the left of me and gestures for me to do the same on the opposite one.

"I'm okay standing thanks."

"Oh that's right, I forgot how much of a snob you are." Her voice puts my defences up and I fight the urge to retaliate. Shouting back at my mum never got me anywhere, it just seemed to fuel her rage. She fed on my reactions, and I won't let her do the same thing now. She sparks up a cigarette and allows the ash to fall to the floor as she puffs away. At least the smell of smoke masks the putrid smell of mould and dirt. "So, what did you come here for Kayleigh?" She spits out my name with distaste.

"I came here to tell you that I am getting married." I don't know why I decide to go with this line of conversation first. I guess that I am hoping for a positive reaction here to break the ice between us. Sadly for me, positivity is severely lacking in this house.

"Pfft. Married? You want to get married?" She takes the time to look at me and I nod my head. "Then you're a fucking idiot." She takes another puff of her cigarette and then picks a glass up from off of the floor. The liquid is clear, and I can only assume that it must be a glass of vodka, it always was her favourite tipple as she used to say. She doesn't just sip the drink, she gulps it, down in one.

"I didn't come here so that you could judge my choices."

"Of course you did. Why else would you bother to tell me?" Her eyes connect with mine and hold my gaze. She's trying to make me conform to her way of thinking and I won't let her. I need closure, and this is how I am going to get it.

"Because you are my mum. Because I thought that you might like to know that I am getting on with my life. Because I thought that you might have been happy for me….."

"Happy? You think that I would be happy that you are about to throw your life away for some guy who is just going to leave you in the end?" *Don't listen to her Kayleigh, she has no idea what you and Ben have together. Keep strong. Don't let her in.* I embrace the positive voice that is trying to help me battle the nagging, sadistic one whilst my mum continues to talk. "Do you think it makes me happy that some guy has drawn you in and taken hold of your senses? You saw what your dad did. You saw him walk out of here and never look back. You know how much that hurt me, yet you want me to celebrate the fact that you are about to embark on the same journey?" She takes a final puff on her cigarette before putting it out on a plate that has been stained yellow.

"My life is nothing like yours."

"Oh please, don't you dare stand there and tell me how much better than me you are. You're my daughter and I know how your mind works. It's the same as mine. You're fucked, just like me. You're going to crash and burn one day young lady, and when you do, don't come crying to me." There is no remorse in her voice, just pure evil. The coldness that has consumed her for years has left no room for any warmth to seep back in.

"How can you say that? Why would you want me to be like you?" I say, my voice keeping calm even though all I want to do is shout. I want to shout and bawl at her, but it would be a waste of my time and energy, a bit like this whole conversation is turning out to be.

"I have never lied to you Kayleigh, and I don't plan on doing so now just because you are in some ridiculous bubble. A bubble that is going to burst one day."

"Have you heard yourself? You haven't seen me for months, and yet this is how you choose to treat me?" I thought that she might have at least seemed a tad pleased to see her only child, but obviously not. I am starting to think that this was a massive mistake. This isn't going to help me get closure. This isn't going to shut down the dark voice in my head.

"I don't have to explain myself to you, and I don't feel the need to carry on this conversation. I have nothing else to say to you."

"Mum," I start, my bottom lip trembling at her words. "Please don't do this. Please don't keep treating me this way." I allow a tear to escape and I scold myself. I told myself that I wouldn't get upset but I can't control the emotions flowing through me. I have never asked her to stop before, so if this doesn't work, then all hope is lost. She looks at me, surprise crossing her face for a moment before her cold mask slips back into place.

"Look at you, crying, begging, what the hell have you become?" The tears start to fall quicker, and I know that I should leave but I can't make my legs move. "How weak are you? If you're crying now, then just think what you are going to be like when your bloke leaves you. Just think of what a mess you will become then. Hey, when it happens, feel free to pop round and bring a bottle of vodka with you so that we can toast how fucking vile all men are, but until then, leave me the hell alone. You are not my daughter. You are nothing to me. Now get the fuck out of my house." Her venomous tone floors me. The tears are blurring my eyes as I make myself turn and run from the house. I fling the front door open, failing to shut it behind me, and I fly down the front path. Seeing her was a mistake. Talking to her was a mistake. The dark voice resurfaces to reiterate everything that she just said. I don't push it away, I haven't got the energy to. I let it spout its evilness at me as I continue to run back in the direction of my house. I will battle it later. Right now, I have no fight left within me.

Chapter Four.

I stumble through my front door and slam it behind me. My heartbeat is racing, my breathing erratic. I didn't slow down on my journey back home. I ignored the questioning looks from people as I ran past them, tears streaming down my face. The dark, evil voice inside of me continued to haunt me as I let it tell me what a failure I was going to become. All of the bad thoughts that I have tried so hard to suffocate broke through. My mum always had a way of making me think, and feel, the worst. How could I ever have thought that seeing her would have made me better? Why did I think that a drunk woman, who lost any ounce of love for me years ago, would make me feel more empowered? As I take in deep lungful's of air, I move on shaking legs to the hall way mirror. My reflection tells me all that I need to know. I look as horrendous as I feel. Red, puffy eyes and tangled hair make it look like I have been in a whirlwind. I rummage through my bag to locate a pack of tissues that I proceed to open so that I can wipe away the tears staining my cheeks. As I brush the rough tissue against my face, I feel unclean. I feel like I need to scrub away all of the bad that has encased me for so long. One moment, a stupid decision, and I am right back to where I was three years ago. Before Ben. Before I felt any semblance of hope encompass my thoughts. I feel worthless, like my mere existence is a sin. I stand here, a thirty-one year old woman, and I have no sense of worth left in me. My mum has broken me once again, and I fear that this time I won't be able to retrieve my fighting spirit. I never told Ben that I was going to visit my mum. He knows about her, and I have told him about how she used to treat me, but I don't think he realises just how much she affects me, even now.

I drop my handbag onto the floor and I make myself walk upstairs. A shower is what I need. I lift my heavy feet up each step until I reach the bathroom. I turn on the shower, feeling numb. As I undress, I replay my mum's words over and over in my head. *'You're my daughter and I know how your mind works. It's the same as mine. You're fucked, just like me.'* I step into the shower and let the scalding hot water cascade over my skin. The warmth feels good. It stings, but at the same time the stinging is giving me something to focus on. I scrub my skin, washing away the bad of the last hour. I need to get clean. I need to rid myself of the evilness that threatens to overtake me. As I scrub and scrub, I can see my skin turning a bright red, but I can't stop myself. The redness only helps me feel better. I don't know how long I am in the shower for, but it must be a while as Ben comes walking into the bathroom, calling my name.

"Kayleigh?" he asks me as he watches me manically washing my body. "Kayleigh," he says more urgently trying to capture my attention. It doesn't work. I continue to scrub. "Jesus," he says as I feel his hands wrap around my wrists, stopping me from moving.

"No, get off of me," I say as I try to move away from him.

"Kayleigh, stop, it's just me." I look through my blurry eyes to his, which are showing nothing but concern.

"No, I need to be clean, I need to wash it all away…." I am babbling, speaking in riddles. Ben looks at me as if I have gone insane.

"Babe, you're skin…." He looks down at my arms and I follow his gaze. I can see that parts of my arms are bleeding where I have been so consumed by my thoughts.

"Oh god," I whisper, my body starting to shake violently.

"Shit," Ben says as he takes charge of the situation. He turns the shower off, lifts me out and places me on the bathroom floor, wrapping a towel around me. I shiver uncontrollably as I am led, like a child, into the bedroom by him. He sits me down on the bed and kneels in front of me, searching my eyes for answers to the many questions that he must have. "What the hell happened?"

"I....." I close my eyes, my voice faltering. Do I tell him where I was? Do I tell him about the thoughts that haunt me? What if he decides that I am too much trouble to bother with? What if he leaves me and I allow the darkness to take over?

"Kayleigh, please, tell me what's wrong." His pleading eyes bring me back to reality. I am going to marry this man, so I need to tell him something. I just have to make sure that he doesn't see just how badly my mind has been affected by my mum.

"I saw my mum." The words come out as a whisper. The tension in the room heightens as I see Ben freeze. His mouth drops open slightly from my revelation. "It didn't go too well," I confirm, although I am sure that he didn't need me to tell him that. It must be fairly obvious that I have had the day from hell.

"What did she do?"

"She didn't do anything." I still feel the need to hide what she is really like. Telling him about my past is one thing but admitting that she still hates me now is quite another.

"Seriously? You're going to sit there and cover for her? Kayleigh, I walked into the bathroom and found you scrubbing your skin until the point that it was bleeding. I think you better tell me exactly what went on." His voice is stern, something that I haven't heard from him before.

He's normally so gentle with me, so I am surprised by the commanding tone that he is exerting.

"There's not much to say. I told her that I was getting married, she told me that I was worthless and would always be a failure." I shrug my shoulders as if it is no big deal, but Ben can see that she has broken me.

"Oh babe," he says as he pushes my wet hair behind my ears. He cups both of my cheeks, wiping away a few stray tears with his thumbs. "She's a drunk. She doesn't mean what she says." I scoff at his words. He has no idea that she really *does* mean what she says. "Why did you go and see her? Why didn't you tell me? I would have come with you."

"I know that you would have, and that was what I was afraid of." His eyebrows raise in question and I proceed to explain my reasoning. "I was frightened that you would see what she was like and you would run a mile."

"Kayleigh, we have been over this. I'm not going anywhere. I don't know how else I can say this to you." He looks exasperated, and I can see why, but at the same time the nagging voice still won't leave me be.

"I needed to do this by myself," I say, changing tactic. "I was hoping that I would find some closure from seeing her, but there is no hope of ever getting that from her. She has only gotten worse over the years. I need to cut her out completely, if only to save myself from the heartache." I don't add that I also need to save my mind. I don't want him to think that I have totally lost the plot. Ben looks at me with a sorry expression on his face before he takes me in his arms and encases me in a tight hug. I hold onto him and breath in his scent. I take comfort in his embrace. Now that I have calmed down a little, I am able to see things a bit more clearly. My mum is gone. She no longer exists. I have lost her, and I need to look forward. I need to concentrate on not letting myself become like her. I don't want to end up bitter and alone with my thoughts eating away at me for the rest of my life. I am going to have to find another way to rid myself of the doubts, because if I can't, then I am going to end up becoming a mirror image of the woman that I saw today. The woman that no longer holds a place in my heart. The woman that has broken me time and time again. The woman that I once called mum.

Chapter Five.

After my meltdown yesterday, I feel as though I need to show Ben that I am okay. I need him to know that I am stable, and yesterday was just a little wobble. My skin, on my arms, feels sore as my clothes brush against it with each step that I take. I embrace the pain, as it acts as a reminder of the strength that I need to make myself carry on. A reminder that I don't need to become someone that even I would hate. As I enter Ben's offices, I make my way to the reception desk and ask if he is free. The pretty young blonde behind the desk tells me that he is and that I can go on through. I thank her and head in the direction of his office. I walk down a small corridor and stop at the third door on the left. I look at Ben's name on the door and feel proud. He has worked his way up from an office temp to become the office manager within a tourism firm. Being a manager myself, I understand the stress of his job. I am about to knock on his office door when I hear a woman's laughter come from the other side. I freeze just before my hand hits the door, my ears pricked and ready to listen for further signs of a female being in his office. When I hear the laugh again a few seconds later, I start to feel sick. Why would there be a laughing woman in his office? Why would the door be closed? I can see no rational answers to these questions and before I can control myself, I swing open his office door to see two pairs of eyes widen in my direction. Ben looks astounded that I have just burst into his office, and the woman in question looks horrified and as if she has been caught doing something that she shouldn't.

"Kayleigh," Ben exclaims after a few seconds. He stands and makes his way over to me, placing a kiss on my cheek. "What are you doing here?" He seems slightly nervous which only helps to fuel my suspicions. *He's cheating on you Kayleigh. He's a man, it's what they all do.* The nagging voice is stronger than ever, my emotions fuelling its energy.

"I thought that I would surprise you and drop by on my lunch break." I keep my voice light, but inside I am dying. I am slowly being dragged under by my dark thoughts. My eyes are still fixated on the woman sat at Ben's desk and I wonder who she is. I don't have to wait long as Ben springs into action and becomes the gentleman that I know and love.

"Kayleigh, this is Monica, Jerry's wife. Monica, this is Kayleigh, my fiancé." Ben sounds proud as he states who I am.

"Hi," Monica says as she jumps up off of the chair and makes her way over to me, her hips swaying as she walks. "Ben has told me so much about you," she continues as she reaches for my hand and gives it a firm shake.

"Has he?" I ask, wondering just how much he has told her.

"Oh sure, he gushes about you all of the time." She looks pleased with herself. Her plumped up lips spreading into a smile that seems genuine on the outside, but underneath I can sense that it's fake. I take in her styled hair, perfect make-up, designer outfit and her manicured nails. Everything about this woman screams that she has money to burn. "Let me get a look at that ring." Before I can say anything, she has taken hold of my left hand and is inspecting my engagement ring. "Oh, it's just so dainty," she says as she lets go of my hand and turns her hand around so that I can see the massive rock that she is sporting. I have no desire to look at it for long. I don't need flashy rings to show everyone that I am with someone.

"Anyway Kayleigh, it was lovely to meet you but I really must dash." She leans in and places a kiss on my cheek which leaves me shocked. I don't even know the woman and she is acting like we have met before. She then turns to Ben and does the same thing to him, although I notice that she also places her hand on his arm and squeezes slightly. I want to slap her. Who the hell does she think she is? I don't care if she is Ben's boss's wife, she has no right to touch him. "Lovely to catch up Ben. See you soon."

"Bye Monica." Ben has the decency to look uncomfortable as she flounces out of the room, the scent of her over-powering perfume leaving a trail behind her. I look at him expectantly, waiting for him to answer the question that I am hoping I don't have to ask. "Sorry about that, I didn't know that she would be stopping by today." Well, he earns a brownie point for his answer, but it poses a question that I am definitely going to ask.

"Stop by often, does she?"

"About once a week."

"Oh. Why?" To my knowledge she doesn't have anything to do with the business, so why would she feel the need to keep stopping by? Ben walks around his desk and takes a seat, gesturing for me to sit opposite him. I feel slightly miffed that I am being told to sit where she just has, but I need to keep my thoughts to myself somewhat. Ben is probably still trying to figure out my behaviour yesterday, so I don't need to give him another reason to worry about my state of mind.

"Apparently, she wants to get a feel for the running of the place. I have no idea why and it isn't my place to ask. She is Jerry's wife and I'm not about to tell her that she needs to get lost."

"Oh right." I clasp my hands together and grip tightly as I try to expel any thoughts that Ben and Monica are doing anything untoward.

"Kayleigh," he says my name softly, drawing my eyes up to look at him. "You have nothing to worry about."

"I know," I reply a little too eagerly. I forget how well he knows me sometimes. "I guess I'm just a little edgy still after yesterday." It has nothing to do with yesterday, but I would rather he think that it does than for him to realise that I am just being a jealous girlfriend. His smile is soft and I can see that he is still concerned about me.

"Yesterday was hard on you, I saw that when I found you in the shower." I can almost see his mind cascading back to the sight of me furiously rubbing at my skin. I feel guilty that he saw that side of me. Since I have been with him, I have managed to hide any sort of unusual behaviour. I have always been scared about him judging me, and I am scared now. I can't lose him. I would completely fall apart without him by my side.

"I wish that you hadn't seen that."

"I blame your mum."

"Don't say her name. She no longer has the right to be called my mum," I retort forcefully. I don't mean to be so defensive, but I can't let myself focus on her. I need to keep all thoughts of her out of my mind before I really do turn into a younger version of her. Ben nods at me, although he looks a little wary. I need to change the subject and make the conversation light-hearted before I have another breakdown about the last twenty-four hours. "So, I just dropped by to see if you fancied going out for a bite to eat after work?"

"Sounds good. What time are you finishing today?"

"About five-thirty."

"Okay. I will make sure that I am out of here by five and then I can pick you up from your office."

"Great." I smile feeling a warmth start to seep back into the cold that is festering within me. "Well, I better get going." I stand up and Ben does the same. He rounds the desk and takes me in his arms, placing a light kiss on my lips.

"You should drop by my office more often. Maybe next time we could spend our time more wisely," he says with a wiggle of his eyebrows so that I catch onto his meaning. I laugh out loud and playfully swat him away.

"In that case, I'll make sure to come by tomorrow too," I reply enjoying that our conversation is ending on a positive note. "I'll see you later." I walk to his office door and let myself out, only turning around to blow him a kiss before shutting the door. I walk back down the hall way but come to a stop when I feel eyes watching me. I whip my head to the left and let my eyes look through a room that has floor to ceiling glass walls. My eyes come to a stop when I see Monica staring at me. She is in the room with a man which I can tell is Jerry, even though his back is to me, but her gaze is fixed on me. There is no friendliness lurking in her eyes, just a fire that seems to blaze with hatred. I quickly look away and scurry off down the hall way, not stopping until I have made my way back outside. *I wonder why she was staring at me in that way? Maybe she thought that I was someone else?* My rational thoughts are soon over taken by the dark voice haunting me. *She knew it was you. She knows that you're not good enough for Ben. She wants him, and maybe she will get him.....*

"No!" I shout, drawing attention from people walking past as they jump at my sudden outburst. My eyes widen as I realise that I spoke out loud. I put my head down and walk as quickly as possible back to my office. I feel like a fool as I round the corner. The nagging voice is driving me crazy, and I worry that I will never be rid of it.

Chapter Six.

It gets to five o clock and I pack my stuff up for the day, ready to meet Ben outside. I place my handbag over my shoulder and walk out of my office, shutting the door behind me. I say bye to Cecile, who is the receptionist. She smiles as I walk out, but that's about as far as our daily interactions go. I step out of the front doors and am expecting to be greeted by Ben, but there is no sign of him. I pull my phone out of my trouser pocket, but there is no message from him. I expect that he is on his way and just running a few minutes late. I wait on a bench just outside of my offices and watch the world go by. People are rushing out of buildings to get home after a busy work day, horns are honking on the main road in front of me as traffic builds up and people become more impatient by the minute. A car just in front of me has their window open, their music playing loudly. I close my eyes and listen to the music. They are playing Linkin Park's, 'In The End,' and I allow the words to roll over me, each one meaning something to me in relation to my past. My life has been far from easy. I may have Ben now, but I have struggled over time, watching anyone I loved walk away from me. The words resonate so strongly within me that I almost feel sad when the song comes to an end and the music changes to another Linkin Park track. I am lost in my thoughts when I hear my name being called.

"Kayleigh?" Ben says as I turn to look at him, a smile gracing my face at the sound of his deep voice. A smile that quickly falters when I see that he isn't alone. Standing next to him is Jerry, and Monica. Jerry has a genuine smile on his face, but Monica's is fake. I can see that it is taking every ounce of self-control for her to put on an appearance. I don't like her, and I don't like that she has taken an instant dislike to me. I jolt myself into standing up and giving Ben a quick hug before I address Jerry and his wife.

"So good to see you Kayleigh," Jerry says as he takes my hand in his and gives it a gentle shake.

"You too," I reply, finding that I actually mean what I am saying to him.

"Jerry and Monica caught me before I left the office," Ben starts, and I turn my attention back to him. "They asked if we would like to grab some food with them." I can see that Ben is urging me to be polite, something that I would rather not do, but feel that it is my duty to.

"Oh great." I am aware that my glee is slightly exaggerated, but I am taken by surprise, so I am hoping that they all dismiss my reaction.

"Fantastic," Jerry exclaims, rubbing his hands together. Monica just smiles, but again it is false. I wonder what her problem is? "How about we try that new Italian place at the end of the road. I have heard wonderful things about their food."

"Okay," Ben says, gesturing for Jerry to lead the way. He does so, and I take the opportunity to link my arm through Ben's and quietly ask him what is going on.

"Why did they ask to go for dinner with us?" I whisper in Ben's ear, all the while keeping my gaze ahead so that I can quickly plaster a smile on my face if Jerry or Monica turn around.

"I have no idea, but I wasn't about to say no. This could be good for my career Kay. Jerry never asks staff to go for meals with him, so it can only be a step in the right direction."

"Okay. I was just looking forward to it being just the two of us."

"I know babe, but we can do it another night. I'm intrigued to see where this is going to go."

"Hmmm." He's not the only one. I have a sneaky suspicion that this impromptu dinner date was the work of Monica, rather than Jerry. Although, I am struggling to figure out why she would want to do this. What motive could she possibly have? *She wants to see how Ben acts around you. She wants to get inside your head and tear you both apart.* I shake my head, hoping to rid myself of the taunts that have haunted me for most of the day. *She's going to become your friend and then take what's yours. You're just too stupid and naïve to see it. You would rather listen to Ben and take his word for it. Pathetic.*

"Stop," I whisper to myself quietly.

"What?" Ben says, clearly indicating that he heard me muttering.

"I just yawned," I reply feebly.

"Oh right. Try not to do that when Jerry talks during the meal." He's joking with me and I allow myself to relax a little. I don't need to listen to the darkness within. I just need to focus on the here and now and enjoy a meal out with my fiancé, even if his boss and wife are joining us.

We reach the Italian place and are promptly seated at a table by the window allowing me the opportunity to look outside if I get bored at any point during this meal. I take my seat beside Ben and Monica sits opposite me. The waiter hands us our menus and I busy myself by perusing the food that is on offer. My mouth waters at the list of endless decadence and I settle on ordering a pasta dish laced with crispy bacon and a creamy sauce to accompany it. I place my menu down and ask Ben to order me a glass of chardonnay. I'm not a drinker normally, but I feel that I need a little something to get me through this meal with Monica staring daggers at me. As the men put their menus

36

down and start to chat about business I feel uncomfortable. The waiter returns with our drinks a few moments later and then takes our food orders. The men opt for steak dishes whilst Monica chooses a salad dish.

"You're eating pasta?" she asks me in horror as I take a warm bread roll out of the basket that the waiter places on our table. I put the roll on the plate beside me and leave it, suddenly feeling guilty for filling up on carbs before our mains arrive. I'm not normally one to watch what I eat, but I suddenly feel disgusting with Monica questioning my meal choice.

"It sounded good," I reply with a shrug of my shoulders.

"I wish I could be as blasé about my diet," Monica says, a fake cackle omitting from her mouth. "I envy women who don't have to watch what they eat." I fidget on my seat as I see her eyes look to my neck, obviously checking for any hint of a double chin developing. The two men are too engrossed in their conversation about a new brochure for some event they are planning to try and bring in more revenue to be bothered about mine and Monica's conversation. "I would have to spend a couple of hours in the gym if I was so much as to let a piece of pasta pass my lips." Monica tries to keep her tone light, but I can sense her underlying bitchiness.

"I've never really had to worry."

"Really?" she asks, raising her eyebrows at me in surprise.

"It's never really bothered me. I am what I am." I'm trying to act ignorant of her rudeness, but inside I am seething. The voice rears its ugly head and joins in the torment of making me feel inadequate. *She can see what a liar you are. She can see past your ridiculous act of not being worried about how you look. In comparison to you, she looks like a queen.* I resist the urge to tell the voice to fuck off as I am aware that it would look strange if I started blurting random words out loud.

"So, Ben tells me that you work in an office. How long have you been there?"

"Nearly four years."

"And do you enjoy it?"

"Yes, I guess I do."

"I never really thought about an office job. I figured that I would be wasted being stuck behind four walls all day long." Jesus, what is this woman's problem? I get the feeling that no matter what I say, she is going to pick fault with me.

"Well, office work isn't for everyone." I respond as best as I can without being rude. I can't say what is really on my mind as I am aware that it would cause problems for Ben at work.

"I guess not," she replies, a smirk pulling at the corner of her lips. "And do you have any siblings?"

"No." Oh god, please don't ask me about my family. Dread creeps up in my stomach as I pray that she isn't going to try and delve into my life any further.

"Ah, an only child. Used to getting your own way I expect." Her presumption makes me angry. This woman is just being spiteful and I can't figure out why.

Because she wants Ben, that's why.

"And what about your parents, are you close to them?" I struggle to form any words but luckily, I am saved a few moments grace as the waiter arrives with our mains. He places each of our chosen meals in front of us and then leaves us to enjoy what he most probably thinks is a lovely meal, when actually this is more like hell for me. Monica pokes at her salad, eating dainty bits of lettuce leaf which she is clearly not enjoying. She looks to my plate of food

38

and shakes her head slightly. If I weren't watching so closely then I would have missed it. I place a piece of pasta in my mouth, but I take no enjoyment from the taste. It's like chewing on cardboard as my appetite has deserted me.

"I was asking about your parents," Monica starts as she cuts a cherry tomato in half and pops it in her mouth. I clear my throat and take a sip of my wine, wanting the ground to just swallow me up. I place my glass back down and take a deep breath, ready to answer her with a feeble excuse when Ben speaks to her.

"Monica, we have the council coming out tomorrow to discuss the new travelling times with us, I presume that you want to be present at the meeting?"

"Oh," she says, seeming shocked that Ben has addressed her. She quickly recovers and places her knife and fork down. "Yes, I think it would be good to see exactly how these meetings are conducted. What time does it start?" I see Ben take a quick glance my way and he gives me a wink to let me know that he was saving me from answering any questions about my parents. I am immediately thankful to him. I didn't think that he was listening, so it just reiterates that he is always looking out for me. Ben starts to brief Monica about the meeting and tells her the relevant information as I slowly try to make my way through my meal. I manage half of it before I give up, admitting defeat. Monica has completely ruined my evening and all I want to do is go home and forget that she exists. Ben engages Monica and Jerry in a three-way discussion, keeping me out of it, which I don't mind in the slightest. Making meaningless chit chat with these people is the least of my worries right now.

"Well, this has been lovely but Monica and I must be going. We have to be at the Border Rooms in the next hour for drinks." The Border Rooms are a high end corporate facility that only deals with the wealthiest of clients. Jerry and Monica Edwards clearly come under the wealthy category. Jerry pulls his wallet out and throws three fifty pound notes down on the table. "My treat for such a wonderful evening."

"Thank you Jerry," Ben says, standing and shaking hands with his boss before Jerry moves out of his seat and lets Monica out. She proceeds to lean into Ben and place a kiss on his cheek. I recoil in horror as she looks at me whilst she does it, a challenging look in her eyes. I see Ben go stiff and I know that he feels awkward from her actions. "And it was a pleasure to spend some time with you Kayleigh," she says as she reaches her hand out for me to shake, which I do as it would look strange if I didn't.

"Yes. You too," I say through gritted teeth.

"We must set up a lunch date, just us girls." I smile at her suggestion but I have no intention of taking her up on it. Jerry then intervenes and shakes my hand before leading his wife out of the restaurant. I sit back down on shaky legs and drink the remainder of my wine.

"Well, that was awful," I say out loud, expecting Ben to agree with me.

"It wasn't so bad," he says causing me to scoff.

"Really Ben? Were you listening to that woman at all this evening?"

"Okay, she can be hard work, but I think she genuinely wants to get you know you better. She invited you for lunch, didn't she?"

"Yeah so she can interrogate me some more. Honestly Ben, trust me when I say that she doesn't like me."

"Oh don't be so silly." I don't like that he is dismissing what I am saying.

"I am telling you that she has a problem with me, I just don't know why."

"You're being paranoid. You don't think anyone likes you." I am shocked at his reply, astounded that he has said it.

"I'm not paranoid." This is a lie, but I don't want him to think that I am crazy.

"Kayleigh, you have always been down on yourself. You need to let go of all the negative shit and see that people do want to get to know you. They don't always have an ulterior motive either." I process his words, each one of them cutting me like a knife. Has he always thought this about me?

"I may have my faults, but I am not imagining this Ben. She doesn't like me and you won't convince me otherwise." I will not back down here. I know when I am right.

"You know what, I don't really want to have this conversation right now. We've had a nice meal so could you at least wait until tomorrow to pick fault with it?" He drains his beer and stands up, buttoning his suit jacket before stepping away from the table and making his way towards the exit. I sit there stunned. Ben has never been like this with me before. *Maybe he is finally sick of your questions and your distrust of everyone. Maybe he is going to run off with Monica and this is his way of starting to distance himself from you. Maybe he has finally realised how good he is compared to you. I bet if he found out the truth about you, then he would be gone before you could blink.* I close my eyes and cradle my head in my hands.

"Please leave me alone," I whisper, pleading with the voice to go away.

"Are you okay Miss?" a voice asks from the side of the table. My head whips up fast and I abruptly stand on my feet and make my way out from behind the table. It's the waiter. He's come to collect the money for the meal and he's been left with a slightly unstable female diner at the same time.

"Yes, yes. Just had a bit too much wine." A lie as I have only had the one, but he graciously smiles at me all the same. I hastily make my way out of the restaurant to find Ben leant against the wall, his hands in his trouser pockets and his head resting back against the wall. I go over to him and his eyes connect with mine. "I'm sorry." I feel that I should apologise for what I said, even if it was the truth. He sighs and pushes himself off of the wall, putting his arms around me.

"I didn't mean to snap. I just get a little frustrated sometimes with the way you are about yourself."

"I know." I agree with him as it is easier than arguing. I don't need Ben as an enemy as well as the rest of the world.

"Come on, let's go home." Ben keeps one arm around my shoulders as we walk in the direction of our house. I rest my head on his shoulder but I find no comfort in his arms tonight. I fear that I am starting to push him away. I need to up my game and go back to hiding my true self. I need to keep the darkness locked away or it is going to steal my future.

Chapter Seven.

I am sat on the sofa, just watching some television after a particularly difficult day at school. The kids in my class hate me. I don't fit in and I don't think that I ever will. They call me names, taunt me, and make me feel like I am the weirdo of the whole school. I thought that I would make friends at high school, but it turns out that I was wrong. I take comfort in the tub of ice-cream that is sat in my lap, the spoon heaped with the honeycomb flavour for me to devour. Food is my escape. For a few moments, it will make me happy. It will make me think that I can get through another day. It sounds stupid, but I will take stupid over the depressing thoughts that threaten to pull me under.

As I focus on the television screen, I try to block out the loud voices coming from the kitchen. My mum and dad are arguing again. It seems like that is all they do nowadays. I already know that mum will be stood there with a glass of wine in her hand, a half empty bottle on the kitchen side. Dad is trying to reason with her about her drinking habits, but she excuses her alcohol consumption with pathetic reasons such as, 'I've had a hard day,' or 'It's my way of unwinding,' or 'It's only the one glass.' I swear that she can't even see what she is doing to our family anymore.

As a young child, my parents were the best. We used to eat family dinners at the dining table, we would watch films together whilst all snuggled on the sofa and they would both kiss me goodnight as they tucked me into bed. Those were the good days. The best. I miss them. Things have changed so much in such a short space of time. It's only been the last year that things have really gone downhill. I have no idea what made mum's drinking worse. I'm just a kid so I don't expect them to tell me the ins and outs of why. Being thirteen years old is hard enough, without having your parents screaming at each other every day. I could already sense that this argument was worse than any of the others that they had had previously. Mum always talked dad round, but I could tell that today it wasn't working.

I turn the television up louder, but there is no way that I can drown out the screams coming from my mum. The sounds coming out of her start to frighten me. I want to run away, but I have nowhere else to go. I wish I had a friend I could confide in, but I don't. I am the outsider. Not only am I the odd one out at school, but I also feel the same way being stuck in this house.

I jump at the sound of a door slamming. I put the ice-cream down on the coffee table in front of me and I quietly get up off of the sofa. With my heart pounding, I walk to the lounge door and peer around. There is no sign of my mum or dad, but I can hear sobs coming from upstairs. I walk to the stairs and make my way up them. That's when my mum starts to plead with my dad.

'Please don't do this. Please don't leave me.' I freeze on the spot at her words, my world suddenly going a bit darker than it was a few moments ago. My dad's leaving? He can't go. He can't leave me here with her on my own. I try to search my brain for an answer to this problem, but at thirteen years old I have no answers. I may be more aware than I should be for my age, but when it comes to my parent's relationship issues I would have no clue where to start. I make my legs move again as I hear a door open which I presume is to my parents' bedroom. As I reach the top, I peer round the banister and see my mum on her knees, begging my dad not to go.

'I can't do this anymore Claire. I can't be with you,' my dad says causing tears to spring to my eyes.

'You can't leave. We have a child together. You need to be here for her.'

'At this point in our lives, the fact that we have a child together is irrelevant.' His words hurt me. They make me feel worthless. My dad doesn't want me? What did I do wrong?

'You can't go John. I love you, I need you.' My mum breaks down, wrapping her arms around his waist as she is still kneeling on the floor.

'Get off me Claire.'

'No.' She's holding onto him tightly. My heart breaks. It is at this point that I watch as my dad tries to get her off of him and things take a nasty turn. They're fighting, something that I have never seen them do before. My eyes widen as I watch my dad throw my mum off of him, her head slamming into the wall behind her. I panic and I race down the stairs and back into the lounge. I hide behind the sofa, my body shaking with what I have just seen. I hear my dad's footsteps as he makes his way downstairs and I hold my breath. I expect him to come and find me, but when I hear the front door open and slam shut a few seconds later I realise that he isn't looking for me. He's gone, and he didn't even say goodbye. My dad has left and he didn't care enough to see me before he went. I start to cry, shock at what has happened causing me to sob loudly. I hear my mum doing the same thing, but I don't go to her. I sit by myself, on the floor and I allow myself to feel the pain and hurt that is building inside of me. My family is broken. I am broken. I am only thirteen years old, but I am broken………

The first weekend that dad was gone was awful. My mum continued to sob. I felt numb. He didn't call, he didn't come and see me. It was like he had just disappeared off of the face of the earth.

I was in my bedroom, led down on my bed, staring at the ceiling when my mum opened my bedroom door and walked in. Her eyes were glazed over so I could tell that she was drunk. I forced a smile, hoping that she would leave just as quickly as she had entered.

'You,' she said, pointing a finger at me. 'You're the reason he left me.'

'What?' I asked thinking that I must have misheard her.

'Your dad left because of you. You always have been a fucking nuisance Kayleigh. Why couldn't you just be a normal kid huh? Why did you have to turn into some sort of freak that no one wants to be around?' Her words hurt. I had never heard my mum being so nasty towards me. I had no idea how to respond. 'Why is it that you have no friends? Why is it that you sit in here festering away every weekend? Why couldn't you just be fucking normal?' I led still, shocked at her outburst. 'You ruined everything,' she sobbed, tears streaming down her face. 'He should still be here. He should still love me, but he doesn't.' At this point she collapsed in a heap on my floor and cried. Her cries echoing through the room. I can't feel sorry for her. What she has just said to me will never be forgotten. Did he leave because of me? Does he not love me anymore? At thirteen, these questions should not be going through my head. I should be out having fun, but instead I am a recluse with no one but myself for company. The sound of my mum vomiting brought me out of my thoughts. I leapt off of the bed and held her hair out of the way as she emptied her stomach all over my bedroom floor.

'Get off of me,' she said once she has finished. She turned her head and looked at me, an evil glint in her eyes. 'I will never forgive you Kayleigh. Just remember that.'

I am being shook, my body moving back and forth rapidly. I hear my name being called, a voice getting louder and louder. My eyes spring open and I momentarily forget where I am. I lash out and try to get whoever it is off of me, but they pin me to the bed so that I can't move. I cry out, shouting for help.

"Kayleigh!" The voice says desperately.

"No…… no you can't do this," I reply needing them to leave me alone.

"Kayleigh, it's just me." I recognise the voice, my brain suddenly triggering into action. "Come on babe, calm down." I stop squirming and allow my eyes to adjust to the darkness of the room. With my body still, the face before me comes into focus and I feel a huge sense of relief flood through me.

"Ben," I whisper, more to myself than to him.

"Yeah, it's just me." His voice is soft in reply.

"Oh thank god." He lets go of my arms and I fling them around his neck, holding him tight to me. He holds me and whispers soothing words in my ear. My body is shaking, my breathing still erratic.

"Are you okay?" he asks me, concern filling his voice. I think his question over for a few moments whilst I calm down my breathing.

"I am now," I whisper, feeling so grateful that he is here.

"You scared me. It took me ages to wake you," he says as he pulls away from me to look at my face. The moonlight from the window streams in helping to mask what I look like. I can only imagine that I look a mess from the nightmare that I was having.

"Sorry."

"You were having some sort of nightmare."

"Was I?" I decide not to reveal all to Ben. He doesn't need to know more about my fucked-up past. He's already seen me freak out this week, so I would like to keep this episode to a minimum. "I don't remember a thing."

"Really?" I nod my head in response. I hate lying to him but telling him the truth could be worse. He could start questioning his decision to be with me. Before he can ask me anything else, I pull him towards me and I place my lips on his. It doesn't take long for his body to relax against mine. I need to distract him, and I need to feel wanted right now. I need to forget, if only for a short while.....

Chapter Eight.

I walk into work the next day feeling completely wiped out. The nightmare from last night is still haunting me. Seeing my mum has brought up so many feelings that I thought that I had hidden in a box at the back of my mind. I need to erase her. I need to keep the memories locked away. I walk past the reception desk and make my way to my office but before I can get there my boss Mr Harvey calls me into his office. I groan quietly wondering what I could possibly have done wrong. People only get called into his office when they are in trouble. I plaster a smile on my face as he stands in his office doorway, his pudgy face giving nothing away.

"Good morning Mr Harvey," I say trying to make my tone as bright as possible. He just grunts and turns to go back into his office. I enter and am told to shut the door behind me. I do so and when I turn around I see that he is not alone. There is a woman with her back to me, sat in front of his desk.

"Take a seat Kayleigh," Mr Harvey says, and I quickly do as I am told. I don't want to be in here any longer than I have to be. I take in the woman's profile as I sit next to her. She's pretty with red hair that is styled in a neat bun. She looks at me, a cute smile gracing her face. She has bright blue eyes and light freckles spreading across her nose and cheeks. I feel a pang of jealousy as I sit here with my lank hair tied back into a boring ponytail. The woman's clothes are designer, a stark contrast to my high street trouser suit.

"I expect you are wondering why I have called you in here," Mr Harvey starts. I don't interrupt, I just nod my head slightly. He doesn't like it when people speak unless he has clearly indicated that they should do so. "Well, I won't beat around the bush as there is plenty of work to be getting on with. I would like to introduce you to Lacey Stone. It's her first day working here and as office manager I would like you to show her the ropes for running the office." I gulp at his words. *Show her the ropes? Is he planning on firing me? The running of the office is my job. Shouldn't I have had a say in this decision? Shouldn't he have given me a bit of warning? And when the hell did he advertise for a new member of staff?* I rack my brains trying to think of anywhere that I may have seen an advertisement for a new job opening, but I honestly can't recall anything.

"Um, Mr Harvey, can I ask a question?" I am aware that I sound nervous as hell, but I need to know if my position is safe within the company.

"Yes." His response is curt. I can tell that he doesn't like that I have something to ask him.

"Well, since when do we need another person to run the office? I don't mean to speak out of turn, but the running of the office is my job." I sit there waiting, the seconds ticking by slowly.

"Kayleigh, may I remind you that it isn't your place to question who I choose to employ. It also isn't your place to ask questions about the running of my establishment." I feel myself blush with embarrassment. Any other boss might have a little sympathy for me and see where I am coming from, but not Mr Harvey. He is notorious for being a hard bastard.

"Sorry sir." I sound pathetic.

"Lacey will be training to help you with the workload if you must know. I am concerned that you are not keeping on top of things lately and bringing Lacey into the mix will take some of the pressure off of you." Now, most people would think that he was doing me a favour, but I am fully aware that he is expressing his disgust at how I have let things slide. I know that I have been a little behind for the last week or so, but I think hiring someone else is a little drastic. It also makes me question how long I have left working here. If she is going to be my replacement, then I would rather know now. Trouble is, I can't ask him outright as he may be inclined to sack me on the spot. "Now, I want you to work with Lacey, show her the daily running, keep her informed at all times. She will share the workload with you and I hope that, between the both of you, things will run a lot smoother."

"Yes sir."

"Lacey will shadow you today and then tomorrow you will start to delegate work to her. Is that understood?"

"Yes Mr Harvey." I sound like a complete kiss ass as I pander to his orders.

"Good. Now, if you don't mind I have things to do." I nod at him and stand up, knowing that is my cue to get the hell out of his office. Lacey looks a little shocked as she stands up and follows me from the office. I open the door and step out, only to stop when I hear Mr Harvey speak again. "Oh, Lacey," he says, and I turn to see her doing the same thing.

"Yes?" she says, her voice sounding much more confident than mine despite her looking appalled at the conversation that just occurred in his office. I don't fail to notice that she didn't address him as sir or Mr Harvey. I cringe as I wait for him to tell her off for not addressing him formally but to my amazement, he doesn't. All he says is, "welcome aboard."

"Thanks," she replies with a smile. I am flabbergasted as she shuts his office door and looks at me expectantly. Her smile soon withers as I stand there, shock written all over my face. "Is there something wrong?" she asks me in a sweet, soft voice.

"Uh….. no, well……." I start blithering like an idiot when I should be the one with confidence here. She is the newbie and I am the experienced one, yet I feel like it is the other way around. *Get a grip Kayleigh.* I shake my head and alter my posture so that I am standing with my back straight, making me appear taller. I have seen people do this and I have seen how it makes others take notice of them. Here's hoping I pull off the look myself. "It's just that, Mr Harvey has a certain way that he likes to be addressed by his staff, but I can teach you the correct way so don't worry about it."

"Oh right, I didn't realise." Lacey starts to look a little worried and I feel a jolt of satisfaction surge through me. *So much for her feeling too comfortable too quickly.*

"So, let me show you my office and then you can get a feel for what it is that I do." I put on a fake smile and turn in the direction of my office. I have to be somewhat friendly to her, seeing as I now have to work with her. I will be keeping my eye on her though as I don't want her to take over my job whilst leaving me blindsided. I enter my office and go to sit at my desk. When I look up I see that Lacey is hovering in the doorway, waiting to be invited in. I gesture for her to take a seat on the opposite side to me and then I take a quick look at my diary. I have a pretty full schedule to stick to which includes working out holiday cover, printing up the new rotas for next week's temps to look at, doing some filing, contacting customers to get their feedback on our newspaper layout, as well as acquiring new advertisers to increase revenue. I switch on my computer and leave my diary open so that I can work through my to do list.

"Is there anything that you would like me to do?" Lacey asks me. She is sitting there expectantly as if eagerly awaiting a task that she can complete.

"Actually, there is. I could really do with a coffee; would you mind making me one?" She looks a little taken aback that I have asked her this question, but she soon wipes the astounded look off of her face and stands up.

"Sure."

"Great. Black with one sugar please. The kitchen is the third door on your left, just down the corridor." I smile at her and wait for her to leave before letting the smile drop from my face. Lacey may seem nice, but I have only known her for five minutes. I have no intention of letting my guard down around her. She will soon hear the office gossips discussing what a recluse they think I am and I am sure that she will be the same as them and eventually ignore me.

Chapter Nine.

I storm through the front door, slamming it behind me. I expect Ben to come running into the hallway to see why I am slamming the door, but the house is silent. *That's strange. He should have been home by now.* I'm later than I normally am after having a bitch of an afternoon at work, so Ben should definitely be home by now. I unzip my handbag and dig out my phone, but I am quickly disappointed when I see that I have no messages or missed calls waiting for me. I quickly dial his number, but it goes straight through to his answerphone. I feel my face pull into a frown. Ben always answers my calls. It doesn't matter if he is in a meeting or not, he never ignores me. *He's with her*, the poisonous voice nestling in my head whispers. A fear slinks its way up my spine as the image of Ben and Monica together enters my head. They are sat at a table in a dimly lit restaurant, his hand holding hers across the table. I screw my eyes shut, digging my palms in to rid myself of the image. *He's starting to see the real you Kayleigh. You can't hide forever.* I struggle to breathe, my lungs feel constricted. *It was only a matter of time before he left you. You're destined to end up alone, just like your mother.* I let out a cry of rage as I hurl my handbag down the hallway, the loud thud of it landing at the other end echoing in the quiet house. *Did you really think that you could keep me quiet? Did you really think that I would let you live a happy life?*

"Shut up," I say loudly, my hands clutching my head as the voice takes a hold of me. *Ben is using you. Ben doesn't love you. No one loves you Kayleigh. Not even your parents want you.*

"Shut up," I repeat, louder this time through gritted teeth. *Ha ha, poor Kayleigh. You thought that you were free but you're not. You're trapped. I'm going to be with you for the rest of your life......*

"LEAVE ME ALONE!" I scream, dropping to my knees on the floor, my legs too weak to hold me up any longer. Red, hot tears fall from my eyes as frustration and anger consume me. The voice mimics me, making me feel worthless. I let out a scream as it continues to tell me that Ben doesn't want me. I thump the floor with my hands, the pain of each hit bringing me a slight comfort, giving me something else to focus on. I am so engrossed in my actions that I don't realise that the front door has opened until I hear Ben shout out my name. At the sound of his voice I come to an abrupt halt and whirl around. His eyes are wide with shock. The air around us becomes tense and I suddenly want the ground to swallow me whole. I feel hot as embarrassment at my actions encases me.

"Kayleigh?" His voice is filled with concern, but I can't bring myself to look at him. *Well, he's definitely going to think that you're crazy now. The truth is coming out.....*

I start to cry again as the voice continues to taunt me. I'm breaking, and I have no idea how to stop it. I hear Ben start to move, his footsteps echoing loudly on the wooden floor. I hang my head in shame not wanting him to look at me. I'm scared of how he will react; my body shakes with the effort it is taking me not to scream out.

"Kayleigh," he says, his voice soft. I shake my head and refuse to acknowledge him. "It's okay babe," he says as I feel his hand touch my arm. I jump a mile from the contact, springing backwards as if he has electrocuted me. I clamber backwards some more until my back comes into contact with the wall, next to the front door. The door is still open and a cool wind sweeps past me. I close my eyes, head still hanging down and I try to reason with myself. It sounds ridiculous, but I need to reason with the voice. I need it to give me a fucking break. My ears prick as I hear the door being closed beside me and then I feel the brush of Ben's arm against mine. I open my eyes and take a look out of the corner of my eye to see that he is sat next to me, his knees drawn up and his arms resting on them.

"I'm here when you're ready to talk." His words flummox me. I expected him to run a mile, but he's still here. He's waiting for me. The thought gives me hope that all is not lost. A slight warmth starts to spread through me, allowing me to take a deep breath and raise my head. I wipe my cheeks with my hands and blow out the breath that I have just inhaled.

"I'm sorry," I whisper, my mouth forming words before I can process them in my mind. "I'm just struggling at the moment. I didn't mean for you to see me like that." I don't need to expand on my answer seeing as he walked in on me losing my shit mere minutes ago. "I don't know what's wrong with me, and I am so scared that you're going to leave." My heart breaks at the thought. Before he came along, I was doing fine on my own. I had learnt to deal with being lonely, but now I am terrified of what I will become if he goes. I place my head back against the wall and look to the ceiling. The minutes tick by as I wait for him to speak. It is agonising, and I am waiting for the voice to return but it seems to have deserted me, for now. I feel Ben's hand on my cheek which causes me to jump slightly. He begins to turn my head to face him, and I don't have the energy to stop him. All of a sudden I feel tired and drained. As my eyes connect with his, I can see that he is worried. His brows are furrowed, and I am pretty sure that his head is trying to figure out what the hell has caused his girlfriend to turn into the mess that is sat before him.

"I think…… I think maybe it is time that you talked to someone." I gulp at his words, my bottom lip trembling and my body tensing. "I'm not saying this to make you feel uncomfortable but it's clear that there is something going on that you are having trouble coping with. I wish that you could talk to me, but I get the feeling that you don't want to."

"It's not that I don't want to, I just can't." I get the words out, but they are so quiet that I am unsure if he has heard me or not. He takes a deep breath, his hand still on my cheek, stroking it gently with his thumb.

"All I know is that since you went and saw your mum, you haven't been the same. I love you, and all I want is for you to be happy."

"I am happy….." My voice fades off as he gives me an uncertain look.

"You don't seem to be."

"I'm just… I need…. I need some time, to process some things." He nods at me and I continue to speak, my voice returning to its normal pitch as my emotions start to level out. "I'm scared Ben. I'm so scared of pushing you away."

"I've told you that I'm not going anywhere." His voice is firm. "I can't keep telling you this only for you to disbelieve it."

"I'm sorry."

"Stop apologising Kayleigh, there is no need."

"I don't deserve you." My eyes lower once again, but Ben isn't going to let me look away from him. He moves himself so that he is knelt in front of me, both of his hands holding my face.

"Look at me," he says, his tone urgent and demanding. I do as he asks, my heart leaping into my throat at what he may be about to say. "I will only say this

57

once more, I am going nowhere." He says each word loudly and slowly. "Tomorrow we will both take the day off of work and we will research some counsellors for you to go and speak to." My eyes widen at his suggestion. "There is nothing to worry about. We will find someone that you are comfortable with and I will support you. I will help you to overcome whatever it is that you are battling. You are not by yourself Kayleigh." His words pierce my fragile heart, bringing me a new hope. "I just want my girl back." I start to sob and he pulls me into his arms, holding me tight against his body. I grip the front of his shirt and I let out all of the frustration that is slowly driving me insane. I cry for the woman that I want to be, and I cry for the woman that I have become. But most of all, I cry for my inability to see through the mist that is clouding my brain more and more with each passing day.

Chapter Ten.

I walk into the office of Clara Meadows, apprehension coursing through me. Ben and I spent the whole of yesterday finding a suitable counsellor, and Clara seemed like a good fit. After a brief chat with her receptionist on the telephone, an appointment was booked for me, and here I am. Ben is holding my hand, pulling me towards the reception desk whilst I remain in a zombie like state. We haven't discussed him walking in on me during my melt down. I don't think he knows what to say and to be honest, if he asked me any questions, I wouldn't know the answers. It's not Ben's place to try to fix my broken mind. I hate that he has seen me so vulnerable. I should be the strong woman that he deserves, but until I can put my issues behind me, I fear that that will never happen. I am only here because I am terrified of losing him. If I don't speak to someone, then I am going to push him away for good, and that would ultimately be the end of me. Ben checks me into the reception and then ushers me to a few seats that are set up in the waiting area, to the right of the reception desk. I sit down and survey my surroundings, trying to distract my brain from what is going to be one of the worst appointments of my life. There are only six chairs in the waiting area, all centred around a coffee table that houses various magazines. A fireplace is the focus of the room, which is on the far-left wall. It is beautiful and has clearly been restored to its former glory seeing as this is an old Victorian building. A large bay window looks out onto a small patio area, with colourful flowers surrounding the small area. Clara obviously takes pride in her workplace looking immaculate and she has definitely succeeded. There is no one else waiting in here with us which makes me feel more comfortable. I don't need people looking at me, judging why I am here. The clock on the wall ticks, the seconds seeming to go by slowly. Seconds that fill me with more and more dread as I await my name being called. I can hear the receptionist tapping away on her computer and I can hear Ben sighing as the minutes roll by. Finally, just when I feel like giving up, the receptionist calls me and tells me that I can go on through to Miss Meadows office. I look to Ben who is smiling at me with encouragement. I smile back, but it is forced. I don't want to be here. I don't want some stranger digging into my life. *Oh god, I need to get out of here. I don't want to lose Ben, but I can't do this. I can't talk about my feelings and shit. If I can't figure them out for myself, then how can some stranger do it for me?*

"Kayleigh?" Ben says with a questioning tone. I look at him and the tears sting my eyes.

"I'm sorry," I say as I rush out of the waiting area, flying through the front door. I run until I am out of sight, stopping around the corner of a building at the end of the road. I can hear Ben calling me, his voice urgent. I hate to worry him, but I can't be near him right now. If I am near him, then he will persuade me to go into my appointment. I will resent him for making me and then our relationship will be so much worse than it is now. I can block out the feelings, I can make them go away, I just need him to give me some time.

"Kayleigh?" a female voice says making me jump and whirl around to see who the voice belongs to. My eyes are wide with fright and the woman stood in front of me is taken aback slightly. "Are you okay?"

"Lacey," I say on a breath, trying to calm my racing heart. "What are you doing?" My tone is accusing, but I can't change it. I can't worry about offending her with my reaction right now.

"I live here," she says pointing to the house that I am stood beside.

"Here?" I question, needing her to confirm it again.

"Yeah," she replies with a nod of her head. I can hear Ben calling my name again and Lacey looks at me questioningly.

"I um….." *I what? What am I going to tell her? That I am here for counselling? That I ran away from my appointment? That I am hiding from my fiancé? That I need a fucking break from my life?*

"Do you want to come inside for a coffee?" she asks, clearly seeing the conflict on my face.

"That would be great," I say with a sigh of relief. Lacey smiles at me and then turns, leading me to the back of her house. I can still hear Ben calling my name and my heart constricts with pain. I hope he can forgive me, and I hope that I haven't done irreparable damage by running away. I will explain it to him later, but right now I need to slow my racing mind. Lacey's timing couldn't have been better, something that I never thought that I would say. I follow her into the back garden and she shuts the gate behind me. Her garden is tidy, mostly lawn with a tiny bit of patio outside of the back door of the house. Her washing is hanging on the line to dry and I notice that her blouses all look so elegant floating in the wind. They hold my gaze and it takes Lacey clearing her throat for me to be broken from my daze. Her kind face smiles at me and then she turns and walks to the house. I follow her once again and am lead into a small kitchen. Lacey goes over to a kettle and fills it with water, placing it back on its stand when she is done and flicking the switch on, so the water can boil. Above the kettle is a cupboard where she pulls out two china cups, depositing them on the kitchen work top. The kitchen may be small, but it is beautifully decorated. Cream walls, black appliances and accessories, and a wooden, pine table that seats two.

"Take a seat," Lacey says, pointing to the table and chairs.

"Thanks." I sit down, no longer able to hear the sound of Ben's voice calling me. It is at this point that I hear my phone ringing in my handbag. I don't pull it out, I know that it is Ben.

"Aren't you going to get that?" Lacey asks as she brings over the drinks and takes a seat opposite me.

"No."

"Okay." She looks a little shocked at my abrupt reply, but I have no reason to explain myself to her. My personal life is none of her business, even if she has been kind enough to invite me in here. "So, what brings you to this part of town?"

"I would rather not talk about it to be honest." I take a sip of my coffee, which she knows how to make from work, and close my eyes at the taste. Lacey obviously has expensive taste when it comes to her caffeine needs. My taste buds are groaning in pleasure as I take another sip and enjoy the feeling of the hot drink sliding down my throat.

"Do you want to talk about what's bothering you?" I can tell that she is trying to get me to open up, but I have no desire to do so.

"Not really." Another few seconds of awkwardness tick by before Lacey speaks again.

"Look Kayleigh, I can see that something is bothering you and if you don't want to tell me then that's fine, but I don't like to see you so upset."

"I'm not upset." She raises one eyebrow at me and I decide to relent, slightly. "I don't mean to be so closed off, it's just been a rough day."

"Well, in that case, why don't we talk about anything other than your day? How about we get to know each other a bit better out of a work setting?" The look of kindness in her eyes makes me feel guilty for being so unsociable.

"Okay. What do you have in mind?" I reply sounding bored.

"Well, what about discussing how dishy Sean is at work." Her eyes go all dreamy at the mention of his name.

"Sean? Really?" My interest is piqued, my tone sounding less bored than it did seconds ago.

"Oh yeah. Have you never noticed how beautiful his eyes are?"

"Can't say that I have." I picture him now, but his face is blurry. I have never taken much notice of Sean, or any of the other guys in the office. When I am in work, I am usually so focussed on my job that I barely pay attention to anyone else.

"Oh Kayleigh, you are really missing out," she says with a wink and a cheeky smile gracing her face. I find myself laughing, the tension within me dissipating. "He took me for a drink after work yesterday."

"Oh?"

"I think he likes me, but I don't want to make a prat of myself. I've only just started working at the paper and I would hate to make a fool of myself and have to look for another job."

"I highly doubt that you would make a fool of yourself. You don't strike me as the stupid type."

"Maybe not, but we all have our weak moments."

"We sure do." I sit there and listen as Lacey prattles on about Sean some more. I take in her words and show interest at the right parts. I watch as she excitedly talks about how Sean makes her feel, and I feel a pang in my chest. I wish that I could be as open as Lacey is being right now, but I have no idea how to. I must zone out because the next thing I hear is Lacey saying my name, questioningly.

"Sorry, I didn't mean to zone out like that."

"It's okay. Did I say something that bothered you?"

"No. I just......." My voice fades off as words fail me. *Why can't I just be normal?*

"Listen, why don't we schedule in some girl's time, outside of work?"

"Why would we do that?" I ask, shocked at her suggestion.

"Because, everyone needs a friend to lean on from time to time." I look at Lacey and she seems so genuine and kind. Can I really put myself out there and make this woman my friend? Can I really trust getting close to another woman when all women seem to do is take an instant dislike to me?

"Why are you being so nice?" I have to ask in order to curb my curious mind. "No one else in the office is nice to me," I say quietly feeling really stupid for voicing it out loud.

"Just because others haven't taken the time to get to know you doesn't mean that I don't want to. We work together, what could be the harm in forging a friendship at the same time?"

Hmm, what could be the harm indeed........

Chapter Eleven.

I walk back through the front door of the house that I share with Ben and I am full of apprehension. I shut the door behind me, ears pricked as I listen for any signs that Ben is here. I can hear the murmur of the television coming from the lounge. Taking deep breaths, I calmly take my jacket off and hang it on the peg by the door. Placing my handbag down on the floor, I proceed to take my shoes off and I roll my shoulders, trying to rid myself of the tension that I am feeling. I spent a further hour with Lacey before I left her house. She was kind and she made me feel as if she really wanted to just be a friend to me, but I won't let my guard down. I don't trust her enough to do that. The only person that I have let my guard down for is Ben, and I now have to hope and pray that I haven't shattered our relationship by running out on him earlier. I slowly make my way down the hall, palms sweaty, breathing laboured. The calmness that I felt seconds ago has left me, only to be replaced by panic and fear. I reach the lounge doorway and peer round, but there is no sign of Ben. I feel a sense of relief that I am being given a few more moments reprieve in which to steel myself for a conversation that I would rather avoid. I turn back to the hall and a loud shriek leaves my lips, whilst my hand clutches at my pounding heart. Ben is stood in the kitchen doorway, and he doesn't look happy. His arms are folded across his chest, his legs widened in a defensive stance and his eyes blaze with anger.

"God Ben, you scared me," I say, hearing the quiver that taints my voice.

"What the hell happened today Kayleigh?" I gulp at his cold tone. Gone is the understanding boyfriend of yesterday.

"I..... I couldn't do it," I whisper, looking to the floor as shame fills me.

"Couldn't do what exactly? You couldn't speak to the counsellor? You couldn't divulge your feelings to her? Or you couldn't face telling me that you are too much of a coward to face up to your issues?" I reel back from his words, the last ones piercing my fragile heart.

"I'm sorry." It's a pathetic attempt at an apology.

"Sorry? You're sorry?" He scoffs at my answer. All I want to do is go to him and have him put his arms around me, but I fear that he will just push me away. "Do you have any idea how fucking worried I was about you? Did you even give a moment's thought to how I would feel when you ran out on me?" I open my mouth to answer, but nothing comes out. "I looked for you for an hour after you left. I was going out of my mind Kayleigh! What the hell is wrong with you? What is it about you that stops you from thinking of anyone but yourself?" He is so angry. Tears start to leak from my eyes.

"I'm sorry," I repeat, but I know that I need to say more. I need to put this right, but my brain won't function. It won't allow me to say the words that I need to.

"Yeah, so you said, but sorry won't work this time. Sorry doesn't mean a god damn thing right now Kayleigh." I risk glancing at him and he looks exhausted. He unfolds his arms, running his hands through his hair and letting out a puff of air. "I have done everything that I can think of to help you. I have been patient with you, I have been considerate of you, but this can't go on." He shakes his head in defeat. "I really thought that today was going to be the start of a new chapter for us."

"I'll rebook the appointment," I blurt out, fear of what he may say next consuming me.

"It's not enough."

"What?" I can hardly get the word out as my throat feels like it is closing in on me.

"I love you, but I can't do this anymore. I can't sit back and watch you destroy what we have."

"Please Ben," I say, sobbing. "Please give me one more chance. I promise that I will go to the counsellor. I promise that I will be better. I promise, I promise, I promise." I repeat the words, desperation evident in my tone. "I can't lose you." I can see him weighing up my words, so I press on, hoping to convince him that I can change. "I need you Ben. You're the only person that has ever really understood me."

"That's not true though, is it?"

"Yes it is."

"No, it's not Kayleigh." Another sigh, another piece of my heart shattering. "You have been pushing me away ever since you saw your mum." The mention of her name has my eyes widening. Ben picks up on this and rolls with it. "It hurts that you can't talk to me about her."

"You don't need to know about how evil she is."

"Maybe I do!" he shouts at me, my eyes flying to his with alarm. "Maybe it will help me figure out what hold it is that she has over you."

"She doesn't have a hold over me," I reply defensively, my back straightening at the accusation.

"You can't even see it can you? You don't even realise that you're doing it."

"Doing what?" I ask the question, but the shake of his head tells me that I won't get an answer. I can see in his eyes that he is done. He's had enough. I've pushed him away.

"I'm not going round in circles Kayleigh. If you can't be honest with me, then we need to end this right here, right now."

"NO!" I choke out, my legs feeling like jelly.

"I'm sorry but, I think that you need to sort yourself out before you can forge a relationship with someone else."

"But, we've been together for three years Ben. We have a great relationship....."

"We did, but we don't anymore." His words leave me speechless. His reluctance to comfort me leaves me cold. "I'm not going to stay here tonight." His words cause my heart to pang so hard that it feels like it is going to burst out of my chest. He leans to the left and bends down to pick something up that is hiding behind the door. When I see that it is an overnight bag, I lose my shit.

"NO! You don't need to leave. We can work this out. We can Ben, I love you." He walks past me and I reach out, my fingers clinging onto his t-shirt as I try to stop him from leaving. "Please," I screech, my emotions rendering me an absolute mess. Ben shrugs me off and I fall to the floor. My knees connect first and send a pain shooting up my thighs, but I welcome it. My eyes are streaming, my nose is running, my body is weak. Ben opens the front door and turns to look back at me.

"I'll be back in a few days for the rest of my things."

"Ben," I say his name and the pain that is obvious in my voice makes my ears hurt. The click of the front door closing behind him has me scrambling to the door, but I hear him get in the car and drive off before I can open it. He's gone. He's left me. I lie my weary body down, my face hitting the cold wood of the floor. *You knew that this was going to happen Kayleigh. You knew that he would leave you one day, just like everyone eventually does. No one can stand to be around you. No one will ever love you enough. No one will ever want a screw up like you.* I stare at the wall in front of me, tears still pouring down my face, and I scream. The sound seeming to echo around the house. A house that is no longer a home. Ben is gone. My strength has left me. I allowed the voice to take over, and I allowed the voice to ruin my happiness. The fucking voice is going to be my downfall.

Chapter Twelve.

I don't know how long I lie on the floor for. The only thing I register is it going from dark to light and then back to dark again. I can't move. My eyes are sore, my head is pounding, and I feel like I am completely lost and there is no way out of the numbness that I feel. My body aches from my position on the floor, but I deserve the pain that I am in. I have driven away the one person that I love, and I need to be punished for that. My eyes are glued to one particular spot of the wall, which has a small black mark on it. I memorise the mark, my eyes following the lines of it, over and over again. A small black smudge that captivates my concentration.

I can hear the sound of rain falling outside, each drip sounding loud in the quiet hall way. I feel cold, my body shivering on the floor but I have no inclination to do anything about it. The house phone has been ringing on and off all day long, but I have ignored it, my body and mind are defeated. Ben is gone, and I have nothing left to make me want to function. My eyes are all cried out and I wait as long as possible before I blink as I welcome the stinging sensation that it inflicts on my eyeballs. Pain takes the heartache away. Pain give me a focus. Pain gives me an outlet to channel my thoughts.

A sudden knock at the door has me lifting my head up and looking towards it, even though I can't see who it is through the frosted glass panels. The first movement of my head in hours. My head feels heavy and it takes every effort to keep it up and off of the floor. The knocking continues and then a voice shouts out, "Kayleigh? Are you in there?" My ears prick at the sweet sound. *Lacey. Lacey is here.* I don't know whether to feel happy or annoyed that she is knocking on my front door.

"Kayleigh?" she calls again, her voice sounding slightly panicked. *She's here to laugh at you. She's here to gloat at the fact that you are on your own.* The voice in my head, which I now realise has been quiet for a while, rears its ugly head. I don't try to fight it, I don't have the energy to. "Kayleigh?" Another shout, and another taunt from inside of me. *She wants to make sure that you are left with nothing. She's like everyone else, you can't trust her.* The knocking stops and I slowly lower my head back to the floor. I can hear that the rain is heavier now. I clear my mind, my inner voice quietens, and I am once again left alone. Alone with my only focus being the mark on the wall.

Chapter Thirteen.

More light and more darkness. Time still passes, and I still haven't moved. I must have nodded off at some point, but I don't feel rested. I don't feel at peace. My inner turmoil is still raging through me. I feel weak and my mouth is crying out for me to get a drink to stop the dryness that coats my throat. I can't hear the rain anymore. I can't hear anything actually. My ears feel like they have had cotton wool stuffed in them, so when I feel a hand gently rest on my arm, I think that I must be dreaming. The hand rocks me a little, trying to gain my attention but I am still focussed on the black mark. It's power over me seeming to have grown with time. I close my eyes and will the rocking sensation to go away. It's starting to make my head spin.

"Stop," I mumble, my voice coming out as a whisper. "Stop it."

"Kayleigh." A voice says my name, but it must be in my head. It can't be real because it's the voice of Ben, and Ben has gone. He doesn't want me. A tear slips from my eye as the cotton wool feeling subsides and I hear his voice as clear as day. "Kayleigh." His voice, so gentle, so loving, and so unlike the last time that I heard him talk. I close my eyes, picturing him actually being here. I picture what was once our happy life together, my dry lips pulling into a small smile, causing them to crack a little. I let my memories lure me in, I let them consume me rather than the black mark on the wall. My inner demons can't taint these memories. They are all that I have left, and I will do everything that I can to protect them. It is the first time that I have felt a slither of happiness in days. As I conjure up the memory of Ben and I moving into our home together, I get the sensation that I am being lifted and that

I am floating through the air. The floating makes it feel like I am in a dream, being taken away from all the heartache. Nothing can ruin this, and if this is a dream and it wants to take me away, then I welcome it. Anything to escape my mind. Anything to escape the feeling of being the freak that is Kayleigh North.

Chapter Fourteen.

The smell of the cigarette smoke hits me first, the rancid aroma penetrating my nose. I screw my face up, even though I know that I will become accustomed to the smell within the next few minutes. I place my school bag down on the kitchen floor and count the empty wine bottles on the side. Three of them, and no doubt a fourth one is glued to my mum's hand. It has been a year since my dad left us, and that year has been a living hell. My mum kept her promise about not forgiving me. She has made me an outcast in my own home. Neither of us have heard from my dad, and I wonder how it is that he can leave me here with a drunk for a mother. How can he just erase me from his memory and act like I don't exist? I have no idea where he is, or if he has started a new life far away from here. I miss him, and I miss my mum.

I walk into the lounge and sure enough there she is, led on the sofa, wine bottle in one hand and a cigarette in the other. The wine bottle is half full, meaning that she is well on track to passing out shortly. It normally takes four bottles for her to be sick and then leave me to clean up the mess whilst she is passed out and oblivious to the misery that I am feeling. She is watching some trash on the television, but when she notices my presence she switches the television to mute and focuses her glazed eyes on me. Glazed eyes that show no emotion. She has a dead look about her, and I wonder for the millionth time if she is just trying to speed up the process of her leaving this world so she no longer has to endure whatever pain it is that is deep within her. I know that my dad broke her, I know that she will never recover, and I know that the day will come when I finally turn my back on her. I haven't even left school yet and I have seen, and heard, far too much.

74

"You're home then," she slurs at me, taking another swig from the bottle.

"Yep." Answers are kept short and sweet to avoid one of her outbursts.

"What fucking kept you out so long?"

"I had an after-school club," I reply. A lie. I don't go to after school clubs, the kids all hate me.

"Waste of time," she scoffs, flicking her fag ash on the floor and making no attempt to use the ash tray that is sat on her lap.

"Do you want any food?" I ignore her comment and ask the same question that I ask every day when I get home from school. "I can cook some pasta."

"Pfft. Again? Can't you be more fucking useful?" We have pasta most nights because I can't cook very much, and we also don't have the money to buy more expensive food due to my mum's need to purchase wine.

"It's all we have."

"Well I don't fucking want any." Her use of the f-word is of no surprise to me. I hear her use it all the time.

"Okay," I say with a sigh and am about to walk out when she speaks again.

"What did I ever do to be lumbered with a fuck-up like you?" I grit my teeth, the insult not a new one but still as painful as the first time that she said it. I don't answer, I just stare at the clock on the wall and wait for her to get her rant over and done with. There is no point running off to my bedroom because she will just follow me. "Look at you, no friends, no prospects, no life. No wonder your dad left. No wonder he wanted to get the hell out of here and never come back. I am ashamed to call you my daughter." I blink back the tears that threaten to break free. Tears will only fuel her more. "You are my biggest mistake. You are

the reason that I am like this. How did I ever raise such a weak human being?"

"Mum, please," I say, my voice quiet.

"Mum, please," she mimics as she pushes herself into a sitting position and drops her cigarette into the ash tray. "God, you sound so whiny." She stands up, swaying for a few seconds before adjusting her position so that she can stay upright. "Nasty, horrible, vile girl." She takes a few steps towards me and the hair on the back of my neck prickles. I can smell the alcohol before she reaches me, its scent seeming to waft over me like perfume. I almost gag. "I hate you Kayleigh," she continues, eyes narrowed, unsteady finger pointing at me. "I really do hate you." My body betrays me as I shake, a lone tear escaping down my cheek. My mum watches it slide down my cheek and then drip from my chin. "Pathetic," she spits and I fight the urge to push her away from me. I fight every instinct that tells me to run far away from this woman. She needs me, even if she doesn't know it.

"Mum, I don't want to fight…."

"You think this is fighting?" A hard look appears in her eyes, one that I haven't seen before and I feel a fear creep up my spine. "I'll show you what fighting is……" I don't hear anything else as her hand connects with my face, a loud sound ricocheting around the room. I'm frozen by her actions, the stinging of my cheek increasing with each second that passes. Tears stream, my last shred of control gone. Another slap follows, I drop to my knees, then a kick. A loud cackle fills my ears, another kick, more pain. A squeal like an animal that is being hunted for the kill leaves my mouth. My hair is being grabbed roughly, a biting sensation going through my scalp from the tugging of the roots. My voice pleading, her voice never wavering, and the voice within me joining in with her. They're both

mocking me. No one is here to support me. I cover my face and brace myself for the next kick to my ribs........

I wake with a start, sweat pouring down my face, panic consuming every part of my body. The room is dark, the shadows coming in from the window leaving me frightened. It takes me a few moments to realise that I was dreaming, memories coming back to me to toy with my fragile state. Bile rises in my throat, burning it in the process. I push it down, not wanting to move anywhere. I look down and see that I am in my bed. I don't remember coming in here. I have no recollection of moving from the hall way floor. My mind is a mess, and I fear that it is only going to get worse the more I let the past take over my present.

Chapter Fifteen.

I groggily walk into the bathroom and use the facilities. The blinding sunshine coming in from the window hurts my sensitive eyes. I squint as I wash my hands and dry them on the soft towel hanging on the rail. I feel awful. Drained, defeated, weak. The nightmare from last night is embedded in the fore-front of my mind. Reliving these memories is breaking me all over again. If I had Ben here, then I would get through this. He would help me. *You wouldn't even have the guts to talk to him about it, so how the hell could he help you?* The voice wakes up within, and it's right. I wouldn't have told Ben. I would have put on a front and crumbled on the inside. I guess that, at least without him here, I don't have to pretend. I don't have to cover up the fact that I am mentally unstable. My legs feel like jelly and I have to hold onto the banister as I make my way down the stairs. I slowly move along the hall way, passing the spot where I led for god knows how long. My eyes automatically find the black mark, the spot that held my attention for so long. A small smile graces my lips and I feel kind of grateful that the small mark kept me busy. I almost laugh out loud at how ridiculous that would sound if I were to tell anyone. I enter the kitchen and am momentarily stunned at the sight of Ben standing at the sink, with his back to me. I close my eyes, shutting them tight as I will my mind not to play tricks on me. My head is a cruel place to be right now. No one would want to trade places with the evilness threatening to make me go insane. I slowly open my eyes and gasp at the sight of Ben still standing there, only this time he is facing me, a concerned look on his face.

"Kayleigh," he says as he makes his way towards me, only stopping when he is a few feet in front. My mouth feels even drier than it did a few moments ago, but the desire to get myself a drink has completely vanished. A lump has formed in my throat, and I wrap my arms around myself as if I am going into protection mode. I opened my heart to this man once and he threw me away, I won't make the same mistake again no matter how much I want to wrap myself around him and never let go. "How are you feeling?" he asks me, his head tilting to the side as if he pities me. I hug myself tighter and wish that I had taken a moment to tidy up my appearance before coming down here. I am well aware that I look horrendous, but then I never expected him to be here.

"I'm fine." My voice is quiet, my throat croaky.

"Would you like a drink?" Ben asks, and I nod my head as my urge to whet my mouth returns. He goes to the cupboard and gets a glass, taking it to the sink and filling it with water before coming over and handing it to me.

"Thanks," I say as I take the glass from him and rapidly devour the contents, the cold water tasting like little drops of heaven on my tongue.

"I think that we should talk."

"We talked the other day," I respond, my voice a little louder now.

"Look," he says as he runs his hands through his hair before letting them hang by his sides. "I may have overreacted." His comment stuns me, my eyes widening a little. "I just….. I…. I'm sorry." He moves closer to me, taking my shaking hands in his. "I should have been more understanding. I didn't even give you a chance to explain yourself and I can't apologise enough." His thumbs rub over my knuckles, the sensation soothing even though I know that I need to be more guarded. "I left you when you needed me the most. I feel awful Kayleigh."

"You do?" My eyes fly up to meet his and the sincerity with which he looks at me chips away at the shield surrounding my heart. My thoughts of keeping it safe disappearing with the blink of an eye.

"I really do. And, when I found you on the floor where I left you three days ago, I knew that what I had done was wrong."

"Three days?"

"Yeah, three days," he says with a nod, clarifying it for me again. I had lost three days without even batting an eyelid.

"Oh god, work are going to be so mad with me…."

"It's okay, I called Mr Harvey and explained that you had been taken ill suddenly and were unable to call in yourself."

"And he believed that?"

"He has no reason not to." I'm sure I'll be called into his office for a warning the minute that I step back into the office, but I can't let myself worry about that now. I have far too much still swimming round in my head to even consider dealing with Mr Harvey.

"Thanks." A genuine smile pulls at my lips and Ben relaxes his shoulders, his arms coming around me as he pulls me to him. A part of me wants to fight it, but it is only a small part. He may have broken me by leaving, but he is back. He has explained why and that is good enough for me. I don't need to protect myself with Ben, something that I had forgotten as I drowned in my own misery. He loves me, and with him back where he belongs, I can start to piece myself back together.

Chapter Sixteen.

Ben insists that I spend the afternoon lying on the sofa and resting. I don't argue with him as he pampers me and caters to my every whim. I can feel the guilt coming off of him in waves, but I try to reassure him that it's all okay. He sits at the end of the sofa with my feet on his lap, his fingers massaging the bottoms of my feet in turn. The television is showing an old black and white film and a thick blanket is covering our legs giving a warm, cosy feeling. Ben thought that it would be a good idea if I got some rest today, before we started to explore why I ran out of the counsellor's office. I agreed, just happy to have him home but something has been bugging me about his change of heart, so I find myself asking the question.

"What happened for you to come back? I mean, you were so angry with me. I honestly thought that you weren't going to speak to me again." He pauses the massaging of my foot and lays his hands on my shin.

"Honestly? Yeah, I was angry but once I had calmed down, I realised that I was being selfish. I also spoke to Monica and she convinced me to sort out whatever was bugging me."

"Monica?" The mention of her name instantly unsettles me.

"She noticed that I wasn't my usual self and wanted to know if she could help in any way." *Oh I bet she did. I bet she helped him real good.* The voice makes me jump as I wasn't prepared for it to start goading me again.

"Did you tell her what happened?"

"God no," Ben says, his eyes going wide. "I just told her that we had had an argument and she said that if I was so miserable then why was I staying away from you."

"Right." A numbness washes over me as I try to keep the jealousy at bay. I don't like Monica, and I know that she has an ulterior motive. One where she plans to take Ben away from me.

"Kayleigh," Ben says, making me look at him. "I didn't discuss what happened with anyone, I promise." Little does he know that that is the furthest thought from my mind. The one pushing its way to the front is the one with Monica in it. *Maybe he did tell her all about my episode? Maybe he is lying to you Kayleigh. You can't trust him, he's just going to leave you.* A tiredness washes over me as I battle to keep the voice away. I can't let Ben see that there is anything else wrong with me. He is already concerned, and if I show any more signs of being unstable, then he may decide to walk out of here again.

"I'm tired," I say, needing to get this topic of conversation over and done with, even if I was the one who brought it up. "Do you mind if I go to bed and get some more sleep?"

"Of course not." Ben gently moves my legs off of his lap and I throw the blanket off of me, moving into a standing position.

"You'll be here when I wake up?" I can hear the uncertainty in my tone and I don't like it one little bit.

"Of course I will." He smiles and I return it, even if I am having to force it. I get to the door when Ben speaks again, stopping me in my tracks. "Hey Kayleigh?"

"Mmm?"

"I love you." Those three words bring a peace to my raging mind. Those three words have the power to keep me on the straight and narrow.

"I love you too," I say before I head into the hall way and make my way upstairs. I have to believe that he loves me, otherwise, what is the point?

Chapter Seventeen.

The room swirls around me as I struggle to keep focussed on anything. The nausea rising in my throat has me clenching my jaw, desperate to keep the contents of my stomach from coming up.

"Well, well, what do we have here?" her voice says, smugness in her tone. I try to turn my head to the side, but the movement of my head makes me feel even worse, so I return to staring at the ceiling, trying to stop it from spinning. I mumble something incoherently. "What mess have you got yourself into now?" her voice is louder and I wish that I could just block it out.

"Please...." I manage to say before I have to stop speaking and clench my jaw once again.

"Please what? Please can I stop being so pathetic? Please can I be the girl that you thought I would be? Please can I stop fucking everything up?" her words ramble on and each one of them sounds like they are pounding on my eardrums. "Or how about please make me normal so that I can fit in with everyone else?" I move my hands to my ears to stop her vile words from entering. I don't need to hear it, I've heard it enough throughout my lifetime. Seconds that turn into minutes pass by and I can feel her steely gaze on me, assessing me, hating me. I wish that I hadn't drank that half a bottle of vodka, but at the time I needed it just to get through my crappy existence. My vision has gone blurry, but I can still make out her figure towering over me. Her unkind face hovering over mine. I register movement to the side of her, but it isn't until I feel her hand connect with my face that I realise it was her arm moving backwards so that she could land an almighty slap on my cheek. The burn of her hit makes me wince, the bile rising

in my throat, her cackle making the hairs on my neck stand to attention…….

I wake with a start and my hand flies to my cheek as if I can almost feel the hit from my dream. My breathing is rapid and my heart is beating wildly, but I breathe in and out slowly, telling myself that she is nowhere near me. I am an adult now and I am no longer under her control. My mum used me as her punch bag, mentally and physically, and I hate that all of the memories have started to resurface. The memories that I should have kept buried but I let crawl back in when I chose to go and visit her a few weeks ago. I lean over to the bedside table and turn on the lamp, my eyes squinting as they adjust to the brightness. I register that the clock says 21:14. I have been asleep for about five hours. I have no doubt that I needed the rest after the week that I have had. My thoughts shift to Ben, and I strain my ears as I listen for any sounds of movement within the confines of the house. I don't want to think that him coming back to me was all a dream. Panic at the mere thought has me racing out of bed and down the stairs, where I hear the faint murmur of the television screen and the low tones of his voice. Relief surges through me and I walk along the hall way, desperate for his arms to hold me and bring me some much-needed comfort.

"I've told you that I am fine Monica." His words stop me in my tracks and I watch as my face pales in the hallway mirror at the mention of her.

"There is no need to worry."

"Yes of course I will be in work tomorrow."

"I'm looking forward to it too." His laughter rings out and seems to echo all around me.

"Don't be silly. You will be fine, and I will be there to hold your hand."

"Sure. I will pick you up at half past two."

"It's no problem. I will see you then." More laughter.

"Bye Monica." I hear him put the phone down on the coffee table. I am rooted to the spot, my mind whizzing at a hundred miles an hour. He was on the phone to her. He's planning to pick her up. Tomorrow. He's going to be alone with her. *See, I told you. You can't trust him Kayleigh, you need to get rid of him. You need to be alone. If you are alone then no-one can hurt you. Don't you see how stupid he is making you look? Don't you get it? Everyone is laughing at you. Poor little Kayleigh. No friends, no life, no future. You are the reason that everyone leaves you. No one can stay with you for long. They all move on eventually. They all see how crazy you really are.* I fly back up the stairs and into the bedroom. I bury myself under the bed covers as if it will bring me refuge from the voice that is taunting me because this time, I recognise the voice that speaks to me. It is a voice that fills me with dread, fear and hate. The one voice that can bring me to my knees and make my world shatter in an instant. That voice belongs to my mum, and she is nestled deep within me, willing me to fail at every possible turn.

Chapter Eighteen.

Sitting at my office desk, I immerse myself in the work that I have missed over the last few days. When I turned on my computer this morning, I was bombarded by hundreds of emails that needed my attention, so that has kept me pretty tied up for most of the morning. I needed to come in today, no matter how much Ben tried to persuade me not to. He thought that I needed some more time to rest, but there is no way that I could have stayed at home knowing that he was meeting Monica this afternoon. My head would have driven me insane had I been alone all day. Not that the voice within me hasn't tried to stir some shit up, but for the time being, I am keeping it at bay.

"Kayleigh," Lacey says as she enters my office without knocking first. I am about to reprimand her, but then I see the concerned look on her face. "Are you okay? I was so worried about you." She takes a seat opposite me, a slight smile on her lips, nothing but sincerity in her voice.

"I'm fine."

"Are you sure? It's just, after the other day, I didn't know what to think...."

"You don't need to think anything Lacey. We had a nice chat the other day, and then I needed some time off of work. It's nothing more complicated than that." My tone is abrupt, a stark contrast to hers but I don't need her prying into my life. It's bad enough that Ben hinted about the counsellor again this morning, let alone having someone at work knowing that I am struggling.

"Oh, right.... sorry. I didn't mean to pry. I'll just go." She stands up and gets to the office door before I call her back.

"Lacey wait," I say with a sigh, knowing that I have been a little too harsh with her. She turns her big, puppy dog eyes on me and I soften slightly. "I didn't mean to be rude, it's just….. it's been a difficult week and I just need to focus on work right now." I attempt a smile but I have a strong feeling that I look deranged, but Lacey doesn't remark. She just looks relieved.

"I understand, but if you ever do want to talk then I'm here."

"Thanks."

"Would you like a cup of coffee?"

"That would be great," I reply as I feel an impending headache creeping up on me. Lacey smiles and flounces out of the office and I watch her, through the glass walls of my office, as she bumps into Sean. Her back is to me, but my focus zeros in on the two of them. The last time I spoke to Lacey, she mentioned that she had a bit of a thing for Sean. If Sean's smile is anything to go by, then I would say that the feeling is mutual. His eyes have literally lit up at the sight of her. I can see him talking and I notice the slight brush of his hand on her arm. Lacey starts to play with her hair, a sign that she is flirting. Sean laughs and I feel a jealousy bubble up within me. It's been a long time since Ben looked at me in that way, and I hate how our relationship is going through a bad patch. I stare, transfixed. Another colleague, Gary, comes up to the two of them and he is soon pulling Sean away. As Sean walks off, Lacey turns to watch him and her eyes are sparkling. Her face is a little flushed, happiness beaming from her. No-one else seems to notice, but I do, and for reasons I can't fathom, I don't like it. She's the new girl here and she seems to be taking over the place. She has her foot well and truly wedged in the door. She has been accepted, whereas I am still an outcast. How can that be? How can she be liked more than me? Why has no-one here ever taken the time to get to know me? *Because they all know that you are evil on the inside. They can all see it. And so will Ben. It's just a matter of time Kayleigh, and the clock is ticking.*

Chapter Nineteen.

I hear the front door close, and I am full of apprehension. How the hell I got through work this afternoon, I will never know. From the moment that the clock showed two thirty, I was beyond useless. My eyes flew to the clock every couple of minutes until the time came for me to leave. The thought of Ben with her consuming me. My mind dreaming up all kinds of scenarios, and none of them work related. Work was not a distraction like I had hoped it would be.

"Hi," Ben says as he walks in the kitchen and comes over to me, placing a kiss on the top of my head. I don't answer him, instead I take a sip of my wine and steel myself for the conversation that I know will probably end with a row. I'm on my second glass of wine, needing the confidence that the alcohol is giving me to enable me to question him. "What's for tea?" he asks as if it is just a normal day. Little does he know that I have rumbled his meeting with Monica.

"I haven't cooked anything."

"Okay. Do you want me to do it?"

"I'm not hungry." At this point, his eyes go to the wine glass and then a look of concern comes over his face.

"Did everything go okay at work today?" he takes a seat opposite me at the kitchen table, and I take another sip of my drink.

"Work was fine." I am not about to tell him that Lacey is planning to steal my job and oust me, I don't need him thinking that I have completely lost the plot. I have come to the conclusion that Lacey is out for herself, and that I need to keep her close, to monitor her every move.

"What's wrong then?"

"Why would anything be wrong?" I say with a tilt of my head, my eyes narrowing.

"I just get the impression that there is."

"Really?" I drag it out, scared to utter the words that I need to say now that it is time to say them.

"Jesus Christ Kayleigh, do we have to do this? Can you not just say what is on your mind and get it over and done with?" Exasperation laces his tone, and I can see that he is tired. Tired of me. Tired of what is happening to us. Panic flares up in me and I down the remaining contents of my glass, needing the alcohol to have more of an effect on me. I take the bottle from the table and pour another glass, filling it to the brim. Replacing the bottle, I sit back and look at the man that I love more than anything in the world. The man that I want to spend the rest of my life with, and I feel crushed that I am having to ask him something that I never dreamed of asking. "Kayleigh? What is it?" Impatience replaces the exasperation. *Just say it Kayleigh. Get it done, and then you can stop prolonging the fact that he will leave you. Get it out in the open, and then you can go back to being alone. All alone, with only my voice for company….*

"Are you sleeping with Monica?" the words blurt out of my mouth, more to shut the voice up than anything else. Ben's face morphs from annoyance to shock.

"I beg your pardon?" A surge of adrenaline rears up within me, and it gives me the courage to ask the question again.

"You heard me. Are you sleeping with Monica?"

"Where is this coming from?"

"It's a simple question Ben, all it requires is a yes or no answer." I keep my face dead pan, folding my arms across my chest defensively.

"Have you lost your mind?"

"That doesn't answer the question."

"NO! Of course I'm not having an affair with her. She's my boss's wife Kayleigh, what the hell is the matter with you?" He's on his feet, pacing the length of the kitchen. I stay sat, watching him, assessing him. *He's lying. He's fucking lying to you. Dig a little deeper. Go on, don't be a pushover.*

"So then tell me, why were you picking her up this afternoon?" That stops him and he whirls on me, eyes blazing mad.

"How did you know about that?"

"I heard you, last night, on the phone." Ben leans down, his palms flat on the table to support him.

"I don't know what is going on in that mind of yours Kayleigh, but you need to put an end to it."

"Why are you dodging the question?" *Because he's a liar. Can't you see that? All men do is cause pain. All they ever do is mess with a woman's emotions and then they leave. Don't be stupid Kayleigh.*

"I'm not dodging, I'm just not answering because it's a ridiculous thing to ask me. Not to mention the fact that you have clearly been spying on me, listening into my conversations."

"I have not been spying. I came down the stairs and heard you talking. I didn't want to interrupt you in case it was important, and that's when I heard you saying that you would pick her up." I shrug my shoulders as if it is no big deal, when really it is a massive deal. This could break us. This could end my relationship with the only man that I have ever wanted. *You might want him, but he wants Monica. It's written all over his face.* I close my eyes, willing the voice to leave me alone and also taking a little comfort from it. It's funny, but the voice spurring me on has given me more confidence to speak my mind. It's the only time that it has ever come in useful.

"I'm going to say this once, and once only. I have done nothing wrong here, and you will not make me feel like I have. You need to speak to someone Kayleigh, and you need to do it sooner rather than later. I can't believe that you could even entertain the idea that I would do something like that. I came back to you, I want things to work between us, but you just keep pushing. It's like you want me gone, and if that is the case then let me tell you, you are going the right way about it." He pushes himself off of the table and walks to the kitchen door way before turning back around to me. "I suggest you figure out what you want, and you do it quickly, because I'm not sticking around to be accused of things that I haven't done. I can't help you if you won't help yourself." With that, he turns and walks away, his footsteps loud in the quiet of the house. I hear the front door close a moment later, meaning that he has once again left me alone. *I told you that he would leave. I told you that you couldn't trust him to be there for you. If only you had listened to me sooner Kayleigh, then you could have saved yourself a world of heartache.* I sit at the kitchen table, feeling numb. I replay everything that was said over and over again in my mind. Each time I replay it, there is one part that sticks out in my mind the most.

'I'm not having an affair with her.'
The words stick out to me more than anything else. I asked him if he was sleeping with her. I never asked him if he was having an affair.

Chapter Twenty.
One month later.

The last month has been a rollercoaster. I've been up and down, and somewhere in between in regard to my mental state. Some days have been harder than others, but I finally feel like I am making some progress.

Sitting in my counsellor's office having just finished my fourth session, I can honestly say that it is helping. I couldn't face going back to the original counsellor after running out of there, so I found a new one. Miss Shelley Lane is forty-three years old and has been a counsellor for the last ten years. From the moment that I walked into her office she made me feel at ease. Something that I desperately needed. I don't feel like she is judging me, unlike everyone else. We have touched upon a few things so far, including my relationship with Ben and my feelings about Monica.

"So Kayleigh, I have booked you in for next week on Thursday at four o clock. Does that work for you?" Shelley asks me.

"Sure."

"Great." She writes the time down on one of her appointment cards and then hands it to me. "If you need me in the meantime, then you know that you are free to give me a call."

"Thanks."

"See you next week." I shake Shelley's outstretched hand and make my way out of her office and to the waiting room. Ben is sat there, flipping through a magazine.

"Hey," I say, coming up behind him and placing my hand on his shoulder.

"Hey." He smiles at me and I can see that he is pleased that I am continuing my sessions. He stands and takes my hand, leading the way out to the car park. We both get into the car, buckle up and then Ben starts to pull out onto the main road. "So, how was it?"

"Good. It was good." Ben always asks, and I always give him the same answer. He doesn't push for any more information and I don't offer any. He doesn't need to know the ins and outs of what I have discussed with Shelley, not least because it is about him and Monica.

"That's great. Do you fancy going and grabbing a bite to eat somewhere?"

"Sure." Things have been so much better between us recently. I haven't mentioned Monica to him again. Instead, I have been pouring my fears out to Shelley. I nearly drove Ben away when I questioned him about his relationship with Monica, and I don't want to do that again. We continue the journey in contented silence and I let my mind wander back to that awful day when I asked if he was sleeping with her. The shock, the hurt, the anger and the disappointment still makes me feel slightly paranoid, but I am pretty sure that I was overreacting. Of course there is still a small part of me that is suspicious, but I am slowly battling the paranoia.

"Where do you want to go to eat?" Ben asks me, interrupting my thoughts.

"You choose."

"How about the Indian restaurant that we like?"

"Sounds good." The smile he gives me makes my heart flutter. He is starting to look at me like he used to, and I love that things are getting back on track between us. The silence resumes, but it's comfortable. I lay my head back on the headrest and close my eyes, my thoughts resuming.

When Ben came back home on that horrible night, he looked beaten. I had done that to him, and in the process, I was breaking myself. I either had to fight or let my life keep spiralling downwards. I chose to fight. I chose to live. No words were exchanged between us as we both tried to battle emotions that were raging through us. Instead of words, we expressed ourselves with our bodies. Ben took me to bed and we made love. Rough to start with, all the aggression coming out before it turned softer, our love for one another taking over. When it was done we just led there, our bodies entwined, our emotions spent. The next morning, I got up before Ben and booked an appointment with Shelley, and the rest is best left in the past. Things have naturally progressed to the point where we are both happier now. We are both fighting for us, and there is no better feeling than that.

Ben pulls into the car park for the Indian restaurant and I exit the car, waiting for him to come around from the driver's side. When he does, once again he takes my hand and leads me. We enter the restaurant and are soon seated at a table near the back. It isn't particularly busy in here tonight, but I am glad that we have been given some privacy by being seated away from the other few customers. The waiter takes our drinks order and hands us each a menu, even though we already know it off by heart. We order the same food each time, so when the waiter returns with our drinks, we are ready to give him our food choices. With that done, the waiter departs and leaves us to it. I take a sip of my lemonade and take off my jacket, placing it on the back of my chair.

"Oh, I forgot to tell you that Mr Harvey has mentioned the possibility of me having to work late tomorrow night to make up for me leaving early today." Mr Harvey is still an ass and he has been less than sympathetic about me having to leave work early once a week for my sessions. I had to tell him about them but thankfully, due to confidentiality, he isn't allowed to tell anyone else.

"How late?"

"I think I should be able to get away at about eight-ish." I'm hoping it will be sooner, but I am also realistic.

"Okay. I'll make sure that I have dinner cooked and then we can relax and put a film on." I smile in response, but the smile is soon wiped off of my face when I hear Ben's name being called.

"Oh, Ben, how lovely to see you," Monica coos at him, her eyes brightening at the sight of him. Ben looks shell-shocked as Monica leans down and places a kiss on his cheek. I sit there and watch as I try to keep myself calm. This is my first test since starting to see the counsellor. If I can get through this without showing any emotion, then it will be a triumph.

"Kayleigh," Monica says, turning to me, her beady eyes shining. "How lovely to see you again."

"You too," I say as we politely shake hands. I let go as soon as I can, not wanting to have to touch her for a moment longer than I have to.

"I hope you're feeling better now?" she tilts her head to the side to show concern, but I see no sincerity coming from her. I glance at Ben who is having the decency to look guilty.

"Yes, much better thank you."

"Oh good. In that case, we must arrange that lunch date that we never got around to." I slightly nod my head but I can think of nothing worse than going for lunch with her. The waiter chooses this moment to come over with our food. I could kiss him for his timing as Monica steps to one side and lets him place the food on the table. When the waiter disappears, Monica takes it as her cue to go.

"Well, it was lovely to see you both. Enjoy your meal." She flashes a brilliant smile, but I can tell that it is forced. There is nothing real about this woman. She sashays away, her hips swaying far more than they need to. Ben isn't paying any attention to her as he is too busy looking at me.

"Are you okay?" he asks me, reaching for my hand across the table and wrapping his fingers around my clenched fist.

"Yeah. I'm fine." It's the first time that we have had to acknowledge that she still exists, and he must be worried that I am about to flip out on him.

"I'm sorry Kayleigh."

"Don't be silly, you didn't know that she would be here."

"I know, but I still feel bad." A look of remorse is written all over his face and I wonder how I could ever have thought badly of him.

"It's fine Ben. She can't get to me anymore, I won't let her. Now, can we just forget that she was here and enjoy our evening together?"

"Yes, I would love that." Ben squeezes my hand one last time before pulling away and tucking into our array of food. I go through the motions of appearing happy, appearing to not let Monica's appearance affect me. I eat my food, I chat to Ben, but I don't enjoy one part of it because the whole time I am battling to keep the voice at bay. The voice hasn't been with me for a few weeks now, but its force to be heard is stronger than ever. I don't need the voice to return. I need the voice to be kept hidden away, and I need to remain strong enough to block it out.

Chapter Twenty-One.

"Kayleigh," Lacey shouts making me turn around to look at her. She's running towards me, her heels clicking loudly on the pavement despite the noise of the early morning commuters. There was a time when the sight of her would have filled me with dread, but now I feel prepared. I have grown closer to Lacey, and I decided that if I were to be friendly with her, then there is no way that she can blindside me and steal my job. We spend most days having lunch together, and Sean has even joined us on a couple of occasions. It's strange when he does, but he is unaware that I know that they are a secret couple so I have to act as if I am as ignorant as the rest of the office is. Lacey has asked me to keep quiet, and I want to gain her trust, so I keep my mouth shut. I need her to feel comfortable enough with me that she doesn't feel the need to take my job off of me when it is eventually offered to her. Mr Harvey has expressed his concerns over my mental state, but he also knows that he can't fire me because of it. However, just because he can't fire me, doesn't mean that he can't set me up or move me to a different department, so if Lacey likes me then she might turn the job offer down and then I can stay exactly where I am.

"Morning Lacey."

"Hey," she says as she struggles to carry several folders that are stacked in her arms.

"Want some help?"

"Please." I take a couple of the folders off of her and carry on walking, Lacey clicking away in her heels beside me. "So, how was your evening?"

"Good. Ben and I went for a meal." I haven't told Lacey about the counsellor. I don't need her to think that I am weak.

"Oh nice, where did you go?" I engage in this small talk for a few moments, but I can tell that Lacey has something else that she wants to divulge. She's like an excited puppy and I almost want to throw her a bone just to see if she will catch it.

"What did you get up to?" I ask, knowing full well that she has been wanting me to ask this the whole time that we have been talking.

"Sean came round to my place and um, well, let's just say that we um….." She blushes and her voice peters off, her eyes going all dreamy like.

"Had sex?" I finish for her. Cue a giggle coming from her like a love-struck teenager.

"Yeah."

"Oh right." I'm not sure what I am supposed to say here seeing as no-one has ever discussed their sex life with me before.

"It was wonderful Kayleigh. I think that things might become more serious between us now." She looks so hopeful, so I refrain from saying that he has probably got what he wanted and will now move on. The cynical part of me thinking that she was stupid to give it up so quickly. Lacey continues to chatter away but I zone out. I don't need to hear about how great he was with his hands, or how he made her feel like the only woman in the world. I am grateful when we reach the front doors of our office block, knowing that she will stop talking once we enter just in case anyone was to over hear her. I push the front door open and make my way past the reception desk and to my office, Lacey still following me. I place the folders down on my desk so that she can pick them up and then be on her way, but she shuts my office door and then comes to sit down, her legs bouncing up and down excitedly. "I mean, I guess that we are now official, but I suppose I need to have the conversation with him. What do you think?"

"Um....." I'm not good at advice, and I am the last person that she should be asking what with the shit storm I have been through in the last few months. There is a knock on my office door which interrupts us. The door opens and Mr Harvey's face appears, and he doesn't look happy.

"Kayleigh, my office, five minutes."

"Okay," I answer, even though he is already leaving.

"Oh shit," Lacey says as the door clicks closed. "He doesn't look too pleased."

"No he doesn't." Panic rises up within me, but I take a few calming breaths so that I can control the emotions that threaten to turn me into a wreck. "I better go and see what he wants." I am already making my way across the office when Lacey speaks.

"I'll come back at lunch and then we can talk some more."

"Sure." This friendship thing is hard, but I need to do it. I need to keep her close. I leave my office and head to Mr Harvey's room, knocking on the door and waiting to be asked to enter. His gruff voice calls out a few moments later and I let myself in, legs threatening to crumple beneath me. I somehow manage to walk to the seat that is opposite his desk and I wait for him to instruct me to sit.

"Sit down Kayleigh." I do so immediately. "I will get straight to the point. We don't have time to waste."

"Okay."

"I have a new project for you to complete."

"Oh?" Now this I was not expecting.

101

"I want you to accompany Sean tomorrow when he attends a meeting for a potential new client. The meeting is at one o clock so it is a lunch appointment. The new client is going to be crucial to our profit margin if they come on board. Sean will lead the conversation, and you will be there to help lure them in."

"Me?" I have never been to an important meeting before. I usually just contact the clients and arrange for someone else to do all of the schmoozing.

"Yes Kayleigh. Now, I realise that this is the first time that you will be sat in on one of these meetings, and I expect you to pull your weight. There is no room for error, do you understand me?" His eyes are cold, and I can see where he is going with this if the meeting should go wrong.

"Yes sir."

"Good. Make sure that you dress appropriately and just make sure that you secure the client."

"Will do."

"Okay. That will be all." I am dismissed. I quickly leave his office, shock rendering me speechless. This is new to me. I haven't been involved in anything like this before. *This is his way of trying to get rid of you. You fuck up at the meeting and then he can fire you.* The voice gives their opinion and I hate that it confirms what I was already thinking. The fact that the voice has reared its ugly head just shows that my strength has momentarily waned. *Yes, this is yet another challenge for you that you are sure to fail. The façade that you have been putting on can only last so long Kayleigh and let me tell you that it won't last forever. You can't get rid of me. I am a part of you, and I am going nowhere.*

Chapter Twenty-Two.

I spent all of last night going over what may be expected of me during today's meeting. I obsessed over what I should say, what I should do, when I should speak before Ben took me to bed and made me forget about the meeting for a while. He didn't like seeing me so stressed, but this is something that I cannot fail at. I need to prove Mr Harvey wrong. There is no way that he is setting me up just so that he can replace me with Lacey. I won't allow it. Now I am sat here with Sean, waiting for the client to turn up. The important client that Mr Harvey needs us to get to sign with our advertising department. I have been briefed by Sean on what is expected from us so I feel more prepared than I did last night. He has explained that this a new client looking at a new business venture, and she is already very well known within the business world.

The waitress comes over and Sean and I order a cup of coffee each. I don't think that drinking wine would be deemed appropriate by the client, even if it would help me with my nerves and confidence. Our cups of coffee are quickly delivered and Sean asks me if I have any more questions about the meeting. I am about to ask what the clients personal names are, seeing as this has been kept top secret, when the words die on my lips. My eyes widen a little as I see Monica strolling over to us, followed by some young lad who looks way out of his depth.

"Show time," Sean whispers as he stands up, a grin plastered across his face. "Good afternoon Mrs….."

"Monica please," she says cutting Sean off. She places a kiss on Sean's cheek as he holds his hand out for her to shake. As she places her lips on his cheek, her eyes collide with mine. "Well, well, Kayleigh," she says pulling back from Sean and focussing all of her attention on me.

"How lovely to see you again." She holds her hand out and I make quick work of recovering from my shock at seeing her. I shake her hand, even though my skin crawls from the contact.

"Yes, what a pleasant surprise," I reply, my voice sounding nothing like me. A sweet, sickly tone emerges almost making me want to gag. I am still sat down as I don't trust my legs not to give out on me. Sean is looking questioningly, something that Monica picks up on.

"It is such a small world. Kayleigh and I know each other through our husbands. Oh, sorry," she says faking shock. "You're not married, are you? I meant my husband and her partner." She smirks, and I would love the opportunity to wipe it off of her plastic-looking face.

"Oh right," I can see that Sean is wary of whether this is a good thing or a bad thing.

"Yes, Ben is such a wonderful man. You are very lucky to have found such a catch," she says to me as she slides onto her seat, her strong perfume hitting my nostrils and making them flare as they adjust to the aroma. I clench my teeth together. I can't say anything because if I do then it might cost me my job.

"So, Monica," Sean says saving me from responding. "We have a brief outline of what you expect from us but why don't you tell us in more detail."

"Oh darling, there is no need to rush this meeting. Can a lady not order a drink first?" she says, playfully.

"Of course, my apologies." Sean signals for the waitress to come back over which she does so with efficiency. Monica proceeds to order her drink and then allows Bobby, who is the young lad with her, to do the same. It strikes me as rude that she hasn't introduced him to us properly, but I am in no position to say anything.

"So, how lovely is this?" Monica remarks, looking around the plush restaurant which is of course being paid for by us. "You know, this has got to be the best meeting that I have had yet." She chuckles and Sean joins in, playing the part. The waitress brings our coffee's over along with Monica's glass of wine and Bobby's beer shandy. They clearly don't want to be as professional as us but then they are the clients, so I guess they can choose to drink whatever they like.

"Would you like to order some food?" Sean asks, ever the doting employee.

"Eventually, but for now the wine is doing nicely."

"Okay. Shall we talk a bit of business then?

"Oh you do like to get down to it, don't you?" Monica answers Sean with a wink and I cringe inwardly at her flirtatious manner. Sean laughs, no nerves present and he proceeds with our agenda. I listen in, but my mind is elsewhere. My mind has gone to places that it shouldn't, and the voice is waking up. *Look at her, flirting, showing herself up. I bet she does that with all the men. It's probably how she gets them in her clutches, and by then they are suckered in with it being too late for them to escape. Just like Ben.*

"What do you think Kayleigh?" Monica asks me, and I feel my face flush at the fact that she has caught me off guard. She smiles slyly, a clear sign that she thinks that I wasn't listening. I wasn't but I have been briefed enough to know what Sean has just said.

"I think that the projections are great. Our outline shows a clear path of what your expected rate would be along with the schedule of how we would uphold our advertising commitments to you." The smile fades from her face, causing me to feel smug.

"Hmmm. That may be the case, but can you predict how many people it will bring to my business?" She's trying another tactic.

"You know that we can't guarantee sales, but what we can guarantee is a great advertisement campaign. And with a great campaign it will enable you to show that you are prepared to pay for quality," Sean replies, taking the reins again. I can see Monica mulling over our joint effort, and I can see that she has no back-up from Bobby. He looks bored to death and has already finished half of his drink. Monica looks pig sick as Sean continues his pitch, not missing a beat. I actually get a little thrill from seeing her coming undone. She expected to walk in here and hold all of the cards, but she has been sadly mistaken.

The meeting lasts another half an hour before Monica announces that she needs to leave. She stands up and shakes Sean's hand before coming back to me. As she takes my hand, she leans in so that only I can hear her.

"You may have it all figured out here, but don't think that you have it all figured out at home." A sharp intake of breath has me reeling back, and has Monica looking like the cat that got the cream. She doesn't hang around for me to respond, I guess my reaction gave her the answer that she wanted. A few seconds later and she is walking across the restaurant, Bobby trailing behind her. *Oh she's good. She just turned the tables and showed that she does indeed still hold the cards.*

Chapter Twenty-Three.

Returning to the office, Sean and I are immediately summoned to Mr Harvey's personal office. We fill him in on how the meeting went and he seems satisfied. He dismisses us and I make my way back to my office.

"You did good today," Sean says, following me.

"You think so?"

"Yeah, despite Monica clearly trying to wind you up."

"Oh, you noticed that?"

"It was hard not to." I am surprised that Sean paid much attention to Monica's behaviour towards me. "What's the deal with her?"

"I have no idea." I am not about to tell him that she has some sort of soft spot for Ben. Sean has never showed an interest in my life before, it would be hypocritical of him to do so now.

"Well, you handled the situation brilliantly."

"Thanks."

"Fingers crossed that she takes us up our offer." I'm not really assed if she does or not, but I guess it will look good for Sean if she does. I am under no illusion that it will do nothing for my position within the company. I may be office manager, but there is really nowhere else for me to go from there. Sean's position is higher than mine, with him running the advertising section and ultimately securing whatever revenue that he can. He is obviously unaware of Mr Harvey's plan to oust me. "Anyway, I better be getting back to work."

"Okay." With that Sean leaves and I am left to myself, until Lacey comes waltzing in.

"How did it go?" she asks me.

"Okay I think. I'm sure that Sean will give you all the details."

"I doubt it. He's been really weird with me since the other night."

"Oh?" This is news to me. I figured that she was still in her dream-like state over the whole sex with Sean thing.

"I don't know what to think." She flops down in the chair opposite me without being invited to. I hold back from saying anything, needing to keep the friendly vibes going between us. "He's been quiet. Almost like nothing happened between us."

"Huh. That's a little odd seeing as you have both been inseparable for the last few weeks."

"I know." A sadness creeps over her, but I can't feel sorry for her. She's clearly too young to have experienced much heartache. "I want to speak to him, but I don't want him to think that I am going to become all clingy. What should I do Kayleigh?" Here she goes again with the asking me for advice.

"Would speaking to him really be such a bad thing?"

"God yes. What if he tells me that he doesn't want to be with me? What if he decides that he can't deal with me working here and us being a couple?" These thoughts never occurred to me, but now that she has brought them up, I can't help but feel that the working together issue could work to my advantage. "Would you talk to him for me?"

"Me?" I reply, my voice higher pitched than usual.

"Yeah."

"But, he doesn't know that I know about the two of you." Has she gone mad? *Hahaha, I think we both know that she isn't the mad one here.*

"Oh, of course he doesn't." My office phone starts to ring and Lacey takes that as her cue to leave. "Sorry, I shouldn't be pestering you whilst we're at work. Can we go for a drink later? I could really use a someone to talk to right now."

"Well, I don't know how much help I will be."

"Please?" She does a stupid pout and puts on her puppy dog eyes. The phone continues to ring. *This is your chance Kayleigh. This is your chance to get inside her head, see what's really going on in there. Take the opportunity, and don't fuck it up.*

"Sure."

"Great," Lacey replies, relief written all over her face. She leaves and I answer the phone to be greeted by an angry customer. I don't have time to think about anything else other than the person yelling in my ear. The yelling part isn't so great, but the not thinking is. Distraction from Monica's parting words are what I need right now, until I have to deal with the meaning behind them at a later date.

Chapter Twenty-Four.

Lacey and I are sat by the window, in a little wine bar down the road from work. I have a cold glass of sauvignon blanc in front of me, and Lacey has a glass of rose. She has been prattling on about Sean for the last ten minutes, not stopping for breath. I'm trying to feel some sort of sympathy for her, but there is none. She was the one who decided to sleep with him, and now she has to deal with the consequences.

"I mean, I thought that he really liked me." Dear lord. I refrain from rolling my eyes as I think that would only heighten her distress.

"Look Lacey, I'm sure that he will be fine, you just need to speak to him. There is no point going over this because you're just going to drive yourself crazy." I don't add that I should know all about that.

"I just….. oh my god…… there he is," she says, her eyes focussed on a figure behind me. I turn around and see that Sean has just walked in with a couple of guys from work. They arrange themselves in a line at the bar and wait to be served.

"Well, now's your chance."

"What? Here?"

"Yes Lacey, here."

"But, he's with people from work. I can't just go up to him and say 'hey, remember how we had sex the other night? I'm just wondering if you were ever going to bother with me again?'" I let out a chuckle at her straight to the point answer.

"Well I wouldn't quite put it like that. Just ask if you can have a quiet word and that it is work related."

"Really? You think that I should?" I can see that she wants to, and I will do anything to get her to quit whining about him.

"Yes. Go and get it over with. I'll just wait here until you are done."

"Okay. Do I look okay?"

"You look fine." You always do.

"Oh god. Wish me luck."

"Good luck." She won't need it. She seems to fall on her feet no matter what she does. Lacey stands up and makes her way over to Sean. I turn to see how it is going to play out, but it is obvious that Sean is into her just from the way that he looks at her. I watch as Lacey takes Sean to one side and then they are huddled, deep in conversation. I get bored of watching after a few moments and I let my eyes roam the different people in the bar. Most of them have clearly just finished work and are enjoying a drink to unwind. I notice a couple sat near the back, huddled together, the woman facing me, the man with his back to me. The hairs on the back of my neck instantly rise as I recognise the woman as Monica. She hasn't seen me, so I push my chair back a bit more so that I am more hidden from her view should she happen to look over. She's making doe-eyes, laughing and sitting so that her long legs are on display. My attention is so focused on her that I don't take too much notice of the man, until he turns to the side. My breath catches, my heart in my throat, blood pounding in my ears. His side profile is one that I have seen many times, his perfectly shaped nose and strong jaw line one that I have admired for years. His hair is swept to one side, his masculine hands curled around a beer bottle. Hands that have been on every part of my body. I struggle to breathe as he turns around some more, clearly checking that the coast is clear. As his face completely comes into view, I feel numb. Jealousy claws its way through my body, fear taking over any reasoning that I may be trying to hold onto as to why he is sat in a bar with her. Ben turns away, putting his back to the room once again and that is when I see her hand move to cup the side of his face. He doesn't bat her away, he doesn't seem to be bothered about the fact that she is touching him. I can see her speaking, and I wish that I could make out what she is saying but the bar is too loud, and I am too far away. Her hand stays there for several minutes, her thumb moving up and down his cheek. Tears well in my eyes from what I am witnessing. He told me that there was nothing to worry about. He told me to trust him, to believe that he had no interest in Monica in a sexual way. The scene that I am witnessing tells me different. The room feels like it is closing in on me. I need to get out of here, but my legs won't move. I am paralysed, and I need to see how this plays out. Monica removes her hand after what feels like an eternity and then she moves in closer, her breasts almost popping out of her designer dress. My whole being goes cold as her face moves closer to his. My heart beats wildly, thumping harder with every second that passes, and when she places her lips on his, I feel like I am about to pass out. The air leaves my lungs, I let out a silent scream, my body trembles and my mind goes into overdrive. *You wouldn't listen to me would you? You thought that you knew best. Trusting a man, tut tut Kayleigh. Such a foolish mistake to make.* I somehow find the energy to push myself up from my seat and I make my way out of the bar. I've seen enough. The image of Monica kissing Ben is firmly ingrained on my memory. I can hear Lacey calling me, but I don't stop. I push my way out of the bar and, once outside, I run with only the voice to keep me company.

Chapter Twenty-Five.

He's a liar.

He's a cheat.

He's taken you for a ride.

How could you be so stupid?

How could you lose your independence and put your faith in one man?

You should have protected yourself.

You should have learnt from my mistakes.

Did you learn nothing from your dad leaving us?

I warned you not to trust anyone.

I thought that you had listened, but I guess watching me go through all that pain has done nothing to warn you of the danger of falling in love.

Stupid girl.

Stupid girl.

Stupid girl.

The rage coursing through me fuels the voice within. I don't fight against it. I let it speak freely. I know that the voice is right. The voice that belongs to my mum, who had her heart broken, is absolutely right. I cannot contain my anger as I throw things around the kitchen of my home. A home that I share with Ben, the man who has brought my world firmly crashing down around me.

Throw another plate, go on, let the aggression out. You will feel so much better after you have done it.

I listen. I throw a plate at the opposite wall, and the sound of it shattering makes me want to do it again. I throw another, and another, until there are no plates left. I stand there with my chest heaving, looking at the mess that I have created, but it's not enough.

Go and rip up his clothes.

Make the bastard leave here with nothing.
Give him nothing Kayleigh. Nothing.

I run out of the kitchen and up the stairs to our bedroom. I am a frenzy of activity as I start to pull his clothes out of the wardrobe, throwing them all over the place. I am so engrossed in getting his stuff out of here that I fail to hear the front door close. I also fail to hear him swearing at the mess in the kitchen, and I fail to hear him coming up the stairs. I don't notice anything until he stands in the door way of our bedroom, shouting my name.

"What the fuck Kayleigh?" His voice makes me stop and I turn to him, his eyes wide with shock. I shake uncontrollably from the sight of him, and all I want him to do is feel the pain that I am feeling. I want him to experience hurt like he has hurt me.

"Get out," I snarl at him.

"What?"

"Get out of here." I move towards him and he braces himself as I lunge for him. He moves back so that I miss him.

"KAYLEIGH!" he shouts, but it doesn't deter me. I lunge again and my palms slam down on his chest. He grabs my arms and wrestles with me for no longer than a few seconds, but he soon has me restrained. My back is against his chest, my arms folded around me, his hands holding firmly onto my wrists. I struggle to catch my breath and all I want to do is get away from him. His hands have been on her, and it makes my skin crawl.

"Get off of me." I attempt to wriggle away, but I know that it is hopeless. I am going to be kept like this until he decides to let me go.

"No, not until you have calmed down and told me what the hell is going on." I start to laugh like a maniac at him. "Kayleigh, please, you're starting to scare me a little."

114

"Am I?"

"Yeah."

"Okay Ben," I spit his name out in disgust. "You really want to know?"

"Yes."

"How's Monica?" I ask, an evil tone to my voice that even I can hear.

"W... What?" He falters just as I knew that he would.

"How's Monica?" I repeat, playing along for now.

"I have no idea." *Liar.*

"Really? That's strange. I could have sworn that I saw you with her not so long ago."

"Uh, I don't think so." I feel his grip on me loosen and I pull away from him, breaking his hold on me. I stumble to the floor with the force of pulling away from him, but I am soon back on my feet and facing him, both of us wary and defensive.

"Are you actually going to stand there and lie to my face?"

"I...."

"I fucking saw you Ben. I saw both of you, huddled together at the wine bar in town. You know, the one just along the road from my work!"

"I...."

"Don't interrupt me, I haven't finished!" I'm shouting, and it feels great to shout. *Let the bastard have it Kayleigh. Make him worry. Make him fear.* "You had your back to me, so you didn't know that I was there. I went for a drink with Lacey and let me tell you that I had the shock of my life when I saw Monica, fawning all over some guy. I actually felt sorry for the guy, you know, being stuck with her, but then the guy turned around and to my astonishment, the guy was you." I point at him, but I am

115

nowhere near done with my rant. "At first I thought that maybe it was work related, until she placed her hand on your face." I can see the colour drain from him, and he knows what is coming next. "And as if that wasn't bad enough, I then had to watch her lean across the table and kiss you." Each word is like a fresh dagger to my heart, but they need to be said. Ben won't get away with this. I won't let him.

"Listen, it's not what you think..."

"Pah. Of course it isn't. Because everyone goes out for drinks with their boss's wife and lets her kiss them. How silly of me to think that it was anything out of the ordinary." I am not backing down, and there is nothing that he can say to calm me.

"Please, just listen to me."

"NO!" I scream, my hands going over my ears, my eyes shutting tight. "I don't want to listen to you, I just need you to get the fuck out of here." I don't hear any response as I still have my ears covered. I wait for what feels like an eternity before I open my eyes. The blank hall way causes me relief, and disappointment at the same time. For a second, I think that he has just gone downstairs and he will be back any moment now, but that thought is soon dashed when I hear the front door shut and I listen to the sound of his car starting up in the driveway. I run along the hall way, picking up a photo of us on the way. I fly down the stairs and rush for the front door. I pull it open just as I see the back of his car about to pull off of the drive. I don't know if he has seen me, but I can take a good guess at the fact that he has. I don't think as I let out a scream that sounds like an animal in distress. The photo frame flies from my hand, launching across the air and landing on his car with a thump. I watch it bounce twice, before it lands on the ground. He races off, not stopping to see what it was that hit his car. I watch his car until it disappears out of sight, and then my eyes fly to the photo frame. My legs finally give way, the rage leaving me and the hurt taking control again. I land on my knees with a thud and I sob. I bury my face in my hands and I let the tears fall down my cheeks in waves.

You did the right thing.

You don't need him Kayleigh.

You only need me.

It can just be us now.

You have only ever needed me, you were just too stubborn to see it.

I'm the only one who will ever understand you.

The only one who can help you avoid heartache and pain.

I am here.

I told you once before that you couldn't get rid of me.

I'm going nowhere.

Chapter Twenty-Six.

"Where do you think that you're going?" my mum asks me, her eyes glazed over once again. I stand before her, backpack over my shoulder.

"I'm leaving."

"Pfft. And where exactly are you going to?" She takes another swig from the bottle, the glass's she used to use are now surplus to requirements. She drinks so much these days that having a glass doesn't matter anymore.

"It doesn't matter where, just know that I won't be coming back." I can't live here anymore. I can't put up with the daily beat downs and the mental abuse.

"You think that someone else will put up with you for as long as I have? You're delusional."

"It doesn't matter what you think. I'm leaving, and I won't ever be coming back." I mean it, with every fibre of my being, I will never return to this place. There is not one part of this place that holds good memories. She has spent the last few years stamping on them, erasing them. I no longer think about my dad. He left me with her, and for that I will never forgive him.

"You selfish little bitch. After everything that I have done for you, you're just going to leave me here, by myself?" It's the first and only time that I have ever seen my mum panicked at something that I have said to her. I don't plan on entertaining her for a moment longer. She pushed me away, and she made me hate her. I want to be nothing like her, and I fear that staying with her will only make me just as bitter and twisted as she is.

"Goodbye mum." I turn on my heel and walk out, blocking out the expletives that are currently being spewed from her mouth. I walk out of the house and make my way to the bus stop, which is just down the road. I have been

quietly setting up a flat of my own for the last couple of weeks. I may not make good money at my current job, but it has just been enough for me to afford the luxury of renting my own place. I wait for the bus and feel like a weight has been lifted off of my shoulders. She is no longer my responsibility. She is no longer my burden. I only have myself to look after now, and I am going to make sure that I don't let her life choices impact mine. I will become a better woman than her. I have to.

I laugh at the memory, wondering when I became so much like her. My relationship is in tatters, my emotional state shot to bits. The promise that I made to myself has been broken, and I lay the blame at her door, as well as at Ben's. I was doing fine until he came along. I was content with my crappy existence. I could survive on my own. Then he wore me down, weedled his way in, and now I am left with nothing to show for our three years together other than emotional heartache. My battle scars are on the inside, and now I have to try and rebuild my life once again. At this moment in time, I have no idea how I am going to do that. At this moment in time, the only thing that is getting me through is the bottle of vodka in my hand. Vodka is my friend, and so is the voice.

It's just us Kayleigh.
We will be okay together.
We don't need anyone else.

I am not going to argue. I don't have the strength to. I let the voice comfort me as I finish the bottle of vodka and lay my head down on the pillow. Closing my eyes, I drift off to the image of Ben's face, and the sound of my mum's laughter, and her words that whisper to me 'I told you so.'

Chapter Twenty-Seven.
Three days later.

"So Kayleigh, how has your week been?" Shelley asks me as I lie back on the couch, staring at the ceiling. I take a few moments to digest her question. There is so much that I need to say, but I have no idea how to put it all into context. How do I tell her that Ben is a lying cheat? How do I tell her that I smashed up my house as I let rage consume me? How do I tell her that I haven't heard a thing from him in seventy-two hours? *You don't need to tell her anything. You have me. You need no-one else.* I let out a laugh in response. *This isn't funny Kayleigh. Shelley is no better than me. I am the only one that can heal you.* To Shelley it must seem like I am taking some time to gather my thoughts, but to me, I am supressing the urge to answer the voice out loud. Shelley doesn't know about the voice. I can't tell her, she will just think that I am crazy.

"It's been fine." I'm lying, but she won't know that.

"Okay." I hear her scribble something down on her notepad, the sound of the pencil on the paper making me grit my teeth.

"I don't know if I need these sessions much longer."

"Oh?" I can hear the surprise in her voice.

"I'm feeling much better."

"Well, that's great but maybe we should see how things go over the next few weeks." *She just wants your money. This is a business. She's not a friend.* "Why don't you tell me how things are with Ben?" Shelley asks, diverting me away from the topic of me cancelling any future sessions with her.

"I don't want to talk about him." She doesn't respond. She must sense that I am shutting down. I don't need her. I don't need anybody.

"Is there anything that you would like to discuss?"

"Not really." I'm tired. I'm weak. I don't have the urge to carry on with this. I need to get out. I push myself up to a sitting position, keeping my eyes trained on the floor. If I look at her she will be able to tell that I am lying, and I don't need her questioning me. "I need to go. I have to be somewhere."

"But we have another forty-five minutes left."

"Yeah, but I need to leave." I stand up, picking my bag off of the floor and placing it over my shoulder.

"Well, do you want to book next week's session before you go?"

"No thank you." I don't say another word as I walk to her office door. She tries to call me back, but I ignore her. I don't even know why I turned up today. I knew that I wouldn't tell her anything, so I have just wasted my time and hers. I leave the building and walk along the pavement, drowning out her shouts behind me. She can't make me go back and she knows it. The shouts die out after a few seconds and I am left with only the voice to keep me company. I am starting to like the voice. It speaks the truth, something that I always tried to ignore before. I thought that the voice made me weaker, but it actually makes me see things for what they are. I forgo catching the bus home and decide to walk. Ten minutes go by and I hear my phone ringing in my handbag. I take it out and see that Lacey is calling me. She has been a pain in my ass for the last three days. She is the only one that knows about Ben leaving. I haven't told her why yet, but she seems to feel the need to check up on me at every possible moment. Some people may find this sweet, but I just find it irritating. I put my phone back in my handbag and keep walking, rounding the corner and finding that I am already on the street where my house is. I keep my head down and ignore the friendly shouts from the neighbours as I pass. I don't need to put on an act with them. They are probably just wondering what all the shouting was about in my house the other night. I am positive that half of the street heard mine and Ben's argument, but I have no reason to care. Let them think what they like, people come to their own conclusions about things anyway. I reach the path to my house and make my way to the front door. Unlocking it, I walk inside and instantly I know that someone is here. I shut the door behind me and wait to see who is going to reveal themselves. I don't have to wait long as Ben emerges from the kitchen, his hands in his pockets, his eyes looking sad. We just stare at each other for a few moments, and I take in his eyes that have dark rings around them. I see that his posture is hunched, his shame evident.

"Kayleigh," he says in greeting, his voice gravelly, instantly pissing me off.

"Why are you here?" I cut straight to the point. I have no desire to listen to his bullshit like I have done for the last three years.

"I wanted to talk to you."

"There is nothing that you can say that I want to hear." I hang my handbag on the hook by the door and take my shoes off.

"Please," he pleads, but the remorse in his eyes does nothing to soften me.

"We're done Ben. What more is there to say?"

"You have it all wrong about Monica and me. There is nothing going on between us."

"Don't insult me with your lies."

"It's not lies. If you would just listen to what I have to say, then you would be able to see that there is nothing going on." I walk towards him, my posture defiant.

"Excuse me, I want to go and get a drink." He steps to the side and I enter the kitchen, a weird kind of calmness settling within me. I busy myself putting the kettle on to make a cup of coffee. I don't offer him one, he doesn't deserve my hospitality. I feel him behind me before his hand touches my arm and I whirl around, eyes blazing as I shrug his hand off of me. "Don't you dare touch me."

"Please Kayleigh, let me explain things."

"NO!" My body starts to tremble from anger, the calmness that settled over me seconds ago has completely gone. "Who the hell do you think you are? You can't just come in here and expect me to listen to the bullshit that is going to come out of your mouth. I saw you Ben. I saw you kissing her. There is nothing else to be said."

"We can work this out, I don't want it to end like this."

"Tough. You did this to us, you ruined what we had together……"

"Oh come on, you haven't exactly been the most stable person over the last few weeks." I reel back from his reply. Never in a million years did I expect him to try and blame me for him kissing Monica. The look of shock on his face shows me that he clearly wasn't meant to say what he did out loud.

"Get out."

"Oh god, I didn't mean to say that."

"But you did, so get the fuck out of here." *See, he's finally shown what a selfish asshole he is. He's going to blame you for his indiscretions. He can't even be man enough to take responsibility. You should have listened to me sooner. You could have avoided all of this if you had only listened.*

"Please..." I can't listen to him begging again, so I push him. He stumbles backwards looking horrified. "Kayleigh, stop." I don't listen to him. I continue to push him, needing him away from me. I can't believe that I ever let myself love him. I have been so stupid. I can see his lips moving as he speaks, but I hear nothing. I am in a blind rage, my strength even surprising me as I push him again and he falls down, landing in a heap on the floor. I stare at him, breathing deeply, all reasoning gone. I want nothing more than to hurt him like he has hurt me. I need him to feel pain like I have experienced from his actions. As he gets to his feet I charge at him, but he dodges me, his eyes wide and uncertain. I collide with the wall, my palms stinging from their contact with the cold surface.

"You know what, nothing is worth this," I hear him say before he walks past me and continues until he is out of the front door, slamming it behind him.

Good girl.

It's for the best.

I'll look out for you, always.

Chapter Twenty-Eight.

"Wait up Kayleigh," I hear Lacey say from behind me. I fight the urge to roll my eyes as I turn and see her happy fucking face smiling at me. She has two take-away coffee's in her hands and as she reaches me she holds one out. "Here you go." She looks as pleased as punch that she has brought me my morning coffee and I have to put on a fake smile as I take it from her and say thanks. I turn back around and continue to walk down the hall way to my office.

"So, how have you been? You've been a bit quiet over the last few days," Lacey says making me stifle a groan.

"I'm fine." I'm not but the less I tell her the better.

"Are you sure?"

"Yes Lacey," I respond, my tone a little impatient. "Why wouldn't I be?"

"Oh well, I just thought that, what with you and Ben breaking up....." her voice drifts off and I can see that she is a little nervous to be bringing his name up. I bite my tongue, waiting for the anger at the mention of his name to pass over me. It takes a moment, but I retain my calm façade, even if I am raging on the inside.

"Honestly, I'm okay. I've been quiet because I have been packing his things and giving the house a good clean." It's true. I packed Ben's things in boxes two days ago, and I put all of the boxes out on the drive way. I then spent the whole night cleaning the house from top to bottom. I needed any shred of evidence that he ever lived there gone from my sight. I never messaged Ben to say that his stuff was out on the drive way, so that is where it remains. I have no intention of telling him either. If he can't be bothered to come and get it then that's up to him.

He also won't be able to get back into the house as I have already had the locks changed.

"Are you sure?" Lacey says as if she is enjoying prodding me for any information that she can get.

"Jesus Christ Lacey, I told you that I am fine, now will you just stop going on." My tone is harsh but I have zero patience left with her.

"Sorry," she responds quietly. We continue to move in awkward silence. I enter my office and take a seat at my desk, switching on my computer as I do. I need to bury myself in work, to take my mind off of Ben and that slut Monica. *They're probably together now, in bed, shagging like rabbits.* "Yes thank you, I don't need reminding."

"Huh?" Lacey says. My eyes widen as I realise that I answered the voice out loud, rather than in my head. Bollocks.

"Oh nothing, I was just...... reading an email and uh, I guess I'm just venting." I don't sound convincing, but then Lacey doesn't know me well enough to know that I am lying to her.

"Oh, okay. Anything you want me to help with?" she asks as she makes her way to my desk.

"No," I answer abruptly making her stop. I can see that she is judging me, assessing my behaviour. I need to get a grip. The last thing I want is for her to try and delve into my life any more than she already has. "Just ignore me Lacey. I guess I'm just a little tired from the last few days." A sympathetic look crosses her face and all I want to do is wipe it off of her.

"That's okay, break-up's are tough." I grit my teeth together at her words. She has no idea what I am going through, and I certainly don't want her giving me pity.

"Yes well, I'm better off without him."

"If you want to talk about anything, then you know where I am."

"Thanks." It is the only response that I can give. She smiles at me and I have to strain my face in order to return it.

"I guess I better go and check the daily board and see if there is anything that grabs my attention."

"You do that." I wave her away and breathe a sigh of relief when I am on my own. Others may find Lacey kind and caring, but I just find her annoying and stifling. How anyone puts up with her cheery nature all of the time, I really have no idea. My eyes are drawn to her walking across the office and checking the daily notes board. Sometimes I despise the fact that my walls are made of glass. It gives no room to block yourself off completely. As Lacey assess whatever shite is written on the board, I notice Sean walking up behind her. My eyes narrow as he allows his hand to graze her hip, a motion that no one else would think anything of, but seeing as I know that they have had a thing going on, I know different. The change in Lacey's body language is immediate. She arches her breasts out a little bit more, juts her hip to the side and starts to play with a lock of her hair. She couldn't be more obvious if she tried, and yet, no one else is taking any notice of them. Everyone else is going about their work, ignorant of the interactions of their colleagues. Lacey begins to laugh and Sean's eyes roam up and down her body. A jealousy rears up within me. Why the hell does she get to be the one to grab attention? Why does everyone seem to like her? What is it about her that makes her so alluring? Why is it that she seems to have men dropping at her feet? I may have only witnessed Sean's actions around her, but I get the feeling that Lacey has never had any trouble finding a man to keep her cosy at night.

127

She's going to turn them all against you.

She doesn't really want to be friends with you. She's bluffing.

Maybe we should give her a taste of her own medicine?

Chapter Twenty-Nine.
Two weeks later.

"So, how was last night?" I ask Lacey as she takes a sip of her cocktail.

"Oh my god, it was so good," she answers with a great big grin. She looks like she slept with a hanger in her mouth.

"And? Did you talk to him about making things official?"

"No," she replies, the smile momentarily wiped from her face.

"Why not?" I have spent the last two weeks watching Lacey and getting to know as much about her as I can. She has opened up to me and I think she now considers me a good friend. I am the first person that she turns to when she needs advice, and so far I have followed the unwritten rule book of girl code. I have been sympathetic when it has been needed, I have been supportive, and I have done everything possible to gain her trust. It has been challenging, but it has given me a focus. Since Ben's departure, it has given me something to concentrate on. I appear to have opened up to Lacey, but little does she know that I am holding back so much. I don't need to give her any reason to doubt me. If she doubts, then my plan will fail.

"Because it didn't feel right, and we haven't been dating for that long. I mean, what if everyone finds out and things start to go wrong?" Lacey bites her bottom lip as she looks to me for an answer.

"You need to stop over-thinking things. Sean is clearly besotted with you, so why wouldn't he want to make it official?"

"He's a guy Kayleigh. They don't think the same as us."

"No, they certainly don't." My faith in men has well and truly gone. There isn't a man alive that could make me fall for them again. Ben hurt me, and that hurt was enough to last me a lifetime. Lacey reaches out and touches my arm. I clearly haven't masked my face very well as I can see that she feels sorry for me. I shrug her arm off and clear my throat. I need to keep this conversation on her and Sean. If I am to get inside their heads, then I need to be totally prepared. "Do you think that he will say no if you ask him?"

"To be honest, I don't want to rock the boat. We have a great thing going on and I worry that putting any kind of pressure on 'what we are' will cause him to back away. I've heard office rumours, and I don't just want to be known as a notch on his bedpost."

"What rumours?" This is news to me. I have never heard anything, but then again why would I have. No one talks to me, apart from Lacey, and maybe Sean on the odd occasion.

"Well, according to Michelle in marketing, she has known Sean to go with quite a few women only for him to sleep with them and then as soon as they try to take things to the next level with them, he dumps them."

"Oh rubbish." I can't have her doubting him. I need her to forge ahead and get him to commit if I am to succeed. "And you believe Michelle?"

"I have no reason not to." Fuck me this woman is so naïve it is ridiculous.

"Of course Michelle is going to say bad stuff about him, he rejected her when she first started working for the paper." I have no idea if this is true or not, but I need to take drastic action here. I can't have Michelle gaining Lacey's trust. She needs to rely on me, and only me.

"No way!" Lacey looks shocked and I just nod my head at her and give her a knowing look. "But she's married."

"So? That doesn't stop her if you catch my drift."

"But she seems so nice."

"Looks can be deceiving Lacey."

"Wow, they sure can. Thanks for telling me Kay. You're a good friend." A genuine smile crosses my face at this point.

You've done it. You've gained her complete trust and now she sees you as the one who holds all of the answers. Good girl Kayleigh, good girl.

Chapter Thirty.

I return home from my drink with Lacey and revel in the fact that I have succeeded in making her a friend. My smugness is quickly wiped from my face however when I see that there is a woman sat on the steps leading up to my house. I can't see her face as she is looking down, but I can see that she is dressed immaculately. A white pencil dress, black stiletto heels, and a black cardigan adorn her petite frame. An ice cold chill washes over me as I get closer. Her hands are holding a small clutch bag, her long red finger nails filed into sharp points. Expensive jewellery drips from her wrist and neck.

"Kayleigh," her sickly sweet voice says, making my hackles rise. I thought that I had seen the last of this woman. I thought that she was done with ruining my life, but I guess she has turned up to meddle with my emotions some more. I make my legs move up the path way and I come to a stop a few feet in front of her.

"What are you doing here Monica?" I ask in a cold tone. I have no reason to be polite to this woman. She stole Ben from me, and he was weak enough to give in.

"I came to talk to you about Ben." The smile that graces her face holds no kindness.

"There is nothing that you could say to me that I would want to hear, so I wouldn't bother wasting your time." I go to walk past her, but she side steps, stopping me from getting to my front door.

"Now, now Kayleigh, there is no need to be so stand-offish with me. Can we not just talk like two mature adults?"

She's playing with you. She's come here to try and fuck you up even more than you already are. But we're ready for her. She won't beat us.

"Ben is no longer part of my life Monica. You're welcome to him."

"I think that you may have got the wrong end of the stick."

"How so?"

"Well, far be it for me to point out the obvious, but I am a happily married woman." I scoff at her words. Marriage means nothing to the devious bitch. I fold my arms across my chest, needing to defend myself in some way.

"And I care about this why?"

"Because, I can't afford for you to go around slandering my good name."

"I haven't said a word about you."

"Really?" She doesn't look convinced, but then, I really don't care what she thinks. "I find that very hard to believe. I mean, you see Ben and I having a meaningless drink together, you put two and two together and come up with twelve. Do you see what I am saying?"

"Not really," I reply with a fake yawn. Monica chuckles, the sound of her laughter going through me.

"Let me put it into simple terms for you. What I do in my private life remains private and seeing as I am about to sign a big deal with the paper that you work for, I could really do without the hassle of some office worker making things difficult for me." Her eyes are narrowed, her stare cold.

"What I say and do are none of your concern."

"Oh but they are Kayleigh. I mean, just imagine someone getting wind of the possibility of Ben and I having an affair. If that happened, then my life would become complicated, something which I don't have the time for." She places her hand on her chin and taps her cheek with one finger to give the impression that she is thinking of what to say next. She needn't have bothered with the act, I can tell that she has already rehearsed what she came here to say.

"Just get to the point Monica." I don't want to be near this woman for any longer than I have to be. She makes my skin crawl.

"Okay," she says, moving a step closer so that I can smell liquor on her breath. "If I find out that you are spreading rumours about me, then you can kiss goodbye to your job. You can also kiss goodbye to any semblance of a life that you have here. I mean, your existence is pretty shitty as it is, but I can make it a whole lot worse."

She needs to be taken down Kayleigh. We need to make her pay for what she has done. Don't listen to her threats, she won't go through with them. She's like one of those pesky dogs that yap constantly. All bark and no bite.

"Just stay the hell away from me Monica. I want nothing to do with you."

"The feeling is mutual, believe me." She looks me up and down with disgust. "Oh and, just before I go, I would like to say one more thing." I sigh and roll my eyes, wishing that she would just fuck off already. She leans her head in, putting her lips beside my ear. "I want to thank you for pushing Ben away. It turns out that it has worked out quite well for me." I allow my eyes to connect with hers, and I can see the elation running through her. This woman likes to play games, and unfortunately, I have become a pawn in whatever game she is playing.

"Ben really is a fabulous fuck," she says in a whisper before walking off, laughing away to herself as she goes. I inhale sharply, her words slicing me. As her heels clip-clop along the pavement, it takes every ounce of strength in me not to turn around and run after the bitch.

She won't get away with it. We just have to bide our time.

Now that you are listening to me, you will finally see that I can help make you happy.

Monica will pay, but first, you need to keep things on track with Lacey.

There is no room for mistakes here Kayleigh.

Me and you.

No one else.

We'll make them pay.

Chapter Thirty-One.

"What the hell is wrong with you Kayleigh? Where has the woman gone that I first fell in love with?" Ben shouts at me, seeing all of his stuff left outside.

"She died, along with any respect she had for you." He looks incredulously at me, not quite believing that I have been callous enough to chuck his stuff out here.

"Are you crazy?" Pah, if only he knew the answer to that one. He starts to sift through his things, picking out certain items and putting them in his car. I watch, not moving, no urge to help him. I study his body as he works, his broad shoulders stretching, his thick thighs stood slightly apart as he bends over, his ass still as peachy as when I first met him.

"Whatever you may think Kayleigh, I don't deserve to be treated like this. I have the right to come in that house, not be left out here, ferreting around like a dog."

"You lost all your rights when I saw you kissing Monica."

"Fucking hell Kayleigh, it was one little kiss. Just one! I didn't even let it go on for long as I pushed her off of me, but you never gave me the chance to tell you that. All you did was jump to conclusions, and now here we are," he says with his arms spread out beside him. I feel shock from his words, but the voice reminds me that he is clearly just trying to clear his name. It's what anyone would do after being caught. I don't answer him, and I try to push away any doubts that I had about his actions. I can't afford to doubt myself. He cheated on me and that's it. It's that simple.

He did cheat on me, and Monica has just confirmed it. I enter the house feeling deflated, wishing that my life could be going differently right now. Things have changed in such a short amount of time. I should never have visited my mum. She started the ball rolling for things happening that were beyond my control. She brought the voice back into my life. She is the one who brought all of my insecurities back. I was doing fine before I went to see her. Ben and I were happy. We had plans. Plans that now won't materialise. I am filled with anger at her. Anger at Ben. Anger at Monica. But most of all, I am disappointed. Disappointed in myself for letting things get this far. If I had just left my mum alone, then maybe I would still be living in my little bubble, carrying on with life as though I hadn't been traumatised at her hands for years. Before I can really think about what I am doing, I am on my feet and walking out of the house. It's time that my dear old mum got a piece of my mind.

Chapter Thirty-two.

I march forwards, getting soaked by the relentless rain, my fury making me feel invincible. The voice has gone quiet, not uttering a word since the altercation with Monica. I could do with it comforting me right now, telling me that I am doing the right thing, but it doesn't. Funny how the one time that I really need to hear it, it decides to fuck off and leave me to it. I guess I really am alone at this moment in time.

I turn the corner and can see my mum's front door come into view. The porch is lit up by a single bulb, luring me like a fly. Eyes on the light, feet moving quicker, I am stood at the end of her path way in no time at all. I stop my feet from moving as I stare at her front door, letting the memories filter in....

"You're a bitch Kayleigh," she says as I take her bottle of vodka away and pour it down the sink. She is so drunk that she can't get up from the floor, where she fell a few seconds ago.

"Look at me!" she screams as I finish emptying the bottle and place it on the kitchen side, turning to look at her. Her eyes are unfocussed, but there is no denying the hate that shines through them. My mum has no warmth left inside of her, that died a long time ago.

"You are a disgrace. You are just like your fucking sleaze-bag of a father. You have the same rodent eyes as him, eyes that judge me constantly."

"Mum, I'm trying to help you," I sigh, exasperated at this monotonous behaviour of hers.

"Pah. You don't want to help anyone but yourself. You think that I am the reason that you have no friends. You think that I am the reason that you have nothing to

look forward to." Her hand rises up and she points her finger at me, her fingernails dirty from where she hasn't washed for days. "Your father is the reason that you are like you are. He is the one who turned you into a freak. All that talk before he left about wanting to make sure that you stood out from the crowd."

"Mum, please stop."

"No, you need to hear this." I'm sure that I have already heard what she is about to say, but I know that saying as much to her will only fuel the demons inside of her more. "He wanted you to be great, so he put you on a pedestal. He made you think that you were better than everyone else. What he didn't bank on was the fact that you became a freak in your own right. You ruined any chance of happiness with your quirky ways and your daft ideas. Never get above your stations young lady. Never think that you are the best." I block her out as she continues her tirade. As I got older she became jealous of my closeness with my dad. I have no idea why she even had me in the first place. She always wanted to be his top priority, and when she realised that she wasn't, she changed........

My mum has always been against me, but it is her words that stay with me. All of the hate is what fuelled me to come here.

"Kayleigh, I know that you are sleeping, but I need to say this to you, and I know that I am too much of a coward to say it to your face." I hear my dad take a deep breath as I lie with my back to him, pretending to be asleep.

"I'm sorry honey but, I can't keep doing this. I can't keep trying to fix your mother. She is no longer the woman

that I fell in love with all those years ago. What she has turned into is a bitter, regretful woman. I have tried so hard, for so long, and the fight has left me. Your mother has killed any ounce of love that I still harboured for her."
He sighs and I struggle not to turn around and give him a hug. I know that he is hurting, but he needs to realise that I am too.

"I want you to know that, no matter what happens with your mother and I, I will always love you. You are my daughter and I will always keep you with me." I keep my eyes closed as he leans over and places a kiss on the top of my head.....

My dad lied. He didn't keep me with him. When I was younger, I always thought that meant that he would take me with him wherever he went. I thought that he would keep me safe and protect me, just like a dad is supposed to do for their child. But he didn't. He left me, with her. He knew what she was like, and he left me with her anyway.

"Kayleigh, why are you wearing dirty school clothes?" Miranda Cliff asks me as I sit by myself on the bench in the playground. I don't answer her, she doesn't really care why my clothes are dirty. She just wants to pick on me in front of her little gang of bullies. They all stand behind her, and I feel my cheeks start to flush with embarrassment.
"Hey, she asked you a question," says Tom Smith, her number one follower. A finger pokes me, sending me to the side slightly as I was unprepared for it. I hear them all snicker, but I continue to keep my head down. I know the drill. I know that in a few moments they will have fulfilled their mission by making me look smaller than I already feel.

"Is your mum drunk again?"
"Do you have to look after her?"
"You're disgusting."
"You're both disgusting."
"How can you even show your face at school?"
"No one likes you Kayleigh."
"No one wants to be your friend because you stink."
"Weirdo."
"Loner."

The taunts go on for a few minutes until they get bored with my silence, and then they prowl the playground looking for their next victim. No one comes to see if I am okay, not even the lunchtime supervisor. She is too busy drinking her coffee and counting down the minutes until she can go back inside and get away from all the kids. No one cares, and that has been the problem all along.......

The front door opening brings me abruptly back to reality, making me jump at the sudden movement.

"Oh jeez," a male voice says as he takes in my sodden appearance. "I didn't expect to see anyone out here." He slings a bag of rubbish by the front door and leans against the door frame. "Can I help you?" he asks, looking at me questioningly.

"Uh, yeah," I clear my throat and shake away the memories that were haunting me. I need to put an end to this. I need to make a life for myself. "I'm looking for Claire."

"Oh, is that the lady that used to live here?"

"Used to?" I ask, having difficulty understanding why she would have moved when she has been here for years.

"Yeah, she died a few weeks ago. I'm just clearing stuff out of here and giving the place a lick of paint. God knows it needs it……" I don't hear anything else he says as my world has just shifted on its axis. *She's dead? My mum is dead? No, she can't be. I would have heard something, wouldn't I?*

"Miss? Miss?" the man in front of me says urgently, looking concerned by the wide-eyed expression on my face. "Are you okay?" I nod my head, unable to form any words. "Did you know the lady?" I look at him as I assess his question. *Did I know my mother? Did I really know her at all?*

"No," I say before I turn and walk off, the rain still beating down on me.

Chapter Thirty-Three.

I keep walking, not wanting to go home after hearing about my mum's death. The voice has remained quiet, not uttering a single word. As I walk, my mind is full of questions, thoughts and feelings. I have no idea how to process them all at once. I don't even think that I have the strength to process them right now. I pass people on the streets, couples strolling hand in hand, others walking their dogs, and the odd group of teenagers that have found their 'spot' to gather in. I speak to no one and I keep my head down. My feet are in charge here, and it isn't until I look across the road that I see that they have brought me to the street that Lacey lives on. I come to a stop and can see that her kitchen light is on. I step back so that I am flush with a wall behind me, meaning that I am out of the lights that are starting to turn on all along the street as the night draws in. I don't know how long I watch before I see Lacey appear in the kitchen window. My eyes are transfixed as I watch her, getting a glass from the cupboard and filling it up with water. She has a smile on her face and a dreamy expression in her eyes. Her hair is a little ruffled and she runs a hand through it. Her eyes look out onto the street and I almost faint with panic as I think her eyes come to rest on me. I keep still, not wanting to give away any movement. I even hold my breath as I anticipate what she will do if she sees me. Her eyes squint slightly, but then a figure comes up behind her and nuzzles their face into her neck. She soon turns her attention away from the window and to the person who is clearly the reason for her dopey expression and fly-away hair.

I continue to watch as Sean's face comes into view, once he has finished whatever he was doing with her neck. He has a big grin on his face and Lacey brings her hand up to his cheek, cupping it as he turns his head and places his lips on her cheek. She closes her eyes and then turns herself so that she is facing him. I watch as their lips lock, and Lacey's hands find Sean's hair, her fingers entwining with his locks. Sean has his eyes closed, both of them unaware of anything else it seems. I allow my mind to cast itself back to a time when Ben would do the same thing to me…..

As I stand at the kitchen sink, washing up the crockery that I used to cook Ben and I a delicious meal, I feel his hands go to my waist and pull me back against him. I let go of the plate that I was washing, and I allow myself to enjoy his arms snaking around my midriff. He puts his palms flat to my stomach and it causes my sex to give a little stir. Ben nuzzles his nose against my neck, sending a tingling sensation coursing down my spine. Goose-bumps appear on my arms and forgetting that my hands are covered in soap suds, I turn myself so that I am facing him. Ben smiles at me and his lips crash down onto mine. I am lost in the moment as I move my hands to his shoulders, making his shirt wet. Ben doesn't seem to care, and neither do I. No one else exists, nothing can come between us as we devour one another, the thrill of having just moved in together taking over our emotions.

I never thought that the day would come where I finally found my one true love.

I always imagined that I would be on my own, but Ben is like a light in an otherwise darkened mind. He has rescued me. He makes me feel alive in ways that I haven't experienced before.

If it weren't for Ben, then I never would have allowed myself to open up to someone. He may not know the extent of what I have been through in my life but with his support, I am becoming a better person. He's good for me, and I defy anyone who ever tries to take that away............

The tears are rolling down my eyes, thick and fast. Seeing Lacey with Sean has caused a new pain to sear itself through my broken heart. Why does she get to be happy? Why does she get to have something that I don't? It's not that I want Sean, far from it actually, but I don't see why they should be together when my life has fallen apart. I see Sean lead Lacey out of the kitchen, where they disappear from my view. I look to the windows on the first floor, but there is no sign of them. I can only imagine that they have decided to take their action to another room at the back of the house. I wipe the tears away angrily, gritting my teeth so hard that I am surprised that they don't crack from the force of my jaw. Turning on my heel, I head back along the road and in the direction of my house. My empty house. My lonely house. A house that holds no warmth for me anymore.

Chapter Thirty-Four.

Getting back to my house, rage overtakes me. I can no longer keep in the immense anger that I am feeling. I tear through the house, smashing things, pulling anything that I can off of the walls and throwing it to the floor. Pictures, ornaments, crockery, nothing is safe. I scream and shout, giving the rage an outlet. The voice hasn't spoken. The voice has decided to stay quiet, and I feel the need to taunt it.

"Don't you want to fucking speak to me now?" I scream into the darkness. "Don't you want to mess with me some more? Or have you done enough? Have you finally decided to leave me the fuck alone now that I have absolutely no one, and nothing to fight for?" I repeat this several times, but as I continue to throw things, I get no answer. The silence makes me angrier. I run up the stairs, after smashing as much as possible downstairs, and I start on the bathroom. Soaps, body washes, shampoos, cleaning products go flying everywhere. I don't care about the mess. I don't care about the destruction. Destruction feels good. It helps my heart a little, giving me a release. My bedroom comes next, and as I rip the bed sheets that Ben has shared with me, I cry. I cry for all that I have lost, and I cry for the mum that I never really knew. As my strength starts to leave me, I sit amongst the shredded sheets and sob. Speaking to my mum was going to be the thing that helped me. I needed to tell her what I really thought, and I needed to hear her reasons for treating me the way in which she did. But I won't ever get to ask those questions now. She's gone, and I didn't even get told.

"Why?" I say quietly. "Why me? Why wasn't I ever good enough?" It's what I have always wanted to ask, but I never had the guts to say it. I lay my head down on the ripped sheets and close my eyes, willing the pain to go away. I don't think that I can take much more. I was almost at breaking point before, but now I know that if there is one more thing that gets thrown my way, then I will snap. And not even I want to know what happens when I snap.....

Chapter Thirty-Five.

"Kayleigh?" A male voice says from the door way of my office. I look up to see that Sean is stood there, waiting to be invited in.

"Come in." He strides into my office with an air of confidence.

"I need you to come to a meeting with me this afternoon."

"Oh?" Sean takes a seat on the other side of my desk and sits back, crossing his legs in front of him.

"Mr Harvey wants you to come with me to do a follow up with that Monica woman." His words cause my adrenaline to spike.

"Why?" I reply, making my voice as loud as possible considering that he has just dropped a bombshell on me.

"Because, we gave a good impression the first time and he wants that impression to continue so that we land this contract."

"I really don't think that I am the right person to accompany you this time Sean." I can't go and meet with that woman. The thought of being near her makes my skin itch.

"Well, you will have to be the one to tell Mr Harvey that you don't want to come then." Sean stands up and starts to make his way out of my office.

"Can't you tell him?" Sean stops and turns to face me.

"No way. You know what a pain in the ass he is. I am not putting myself in the firing line."

"Please Sean?"

"Sorry, no can do." I can feel the irritation building within me. I can't believe that Sean won't do this one little thing. After everything that I have been through lately, the last thing that I need to do is piss off my boss. Of course Sean doesn't know what I have been through as I have sworn Lacey to secrecy about Ben but still, he should man up and go and speak to Mr Harvey for me.

"Oh come on Sean, Mr Harvey already has it in for me."

"So don't give him a reason to get on your case. Just come to the meeting."

"I......"

"Look, you don't have to do any talking. I will be the one to charm the pants off of her, you just need to be there to show a solidarity. She clearly liked us last time, so it makes sense for us to be the ones to meet with her again."

"I....." I can't form any words. My mouth has gone dry at the thought of being anywhere near that woman again. She wrecked my relationship, she helped to put doubt in my mind and now I am expected to sweet talk her?

"I'll come by at half one to get you and then we can walk to the restaurant," Sean says interrupting my thoughts before he makes a swift exit from my office, leaving me open-mouthed with shock. I watch him as he walks along the hall way, his muscular back rippling with every movement that he makes.

This could be your chance to end them, the voice says making an unexpected return. *This could be your way into Sean's head. Get to know him better, take him away from Lacey. Make her heart break just like yours has.*

"Kayleigh?" Another voice, but this one female and this one belonging to Lacey. I shake my head from side to side to rid myself of the voice and I lean back in my chair.

"What is it Lacey?" I ask her, a little bit more abruptly than I intended.

"Um, I just heard that you are meeting with Monica this afternoon. Are you going to be okay with that? Do you want me to go instead?" *And there it is, she wants your job. She's trying to make herself look good by taking your place. It won't be long before she has your job, your office, your life. She is a devil in disguise. Don't be fooled by her. Don't let her in Kayleigh.*

"I will be fine," I reply with my shoulders reared back in a defiant posture. I sound more confident than I feel, but I will be damned if I let someone else take a part of my life from me. I have already handed over too much.

Chapter Thirty-Six.

Sitting in the restaurant, waiting for the bitch from hell to arrive feels like some form of torture. The voice has been spurring me on, coaxing me into making Monica feel as small as I do right now. I have no idea how I am going to achieve this, but I guess that I am just going to have to improvise as we go along. I am sat next to Sean, his aftershave wafting around me making me feel a little light-headed. The scent he emulates is a little overpowering, but at the same time it makes me realise how long it has been since I have been this close to a man. It has been weeks. Weeks where I have been without love, without comfort, and without the sense that I have any sexual prowess whatsoever. I blame Ben for inflicting these thoughts upon me. If it weren't for him, I would never have known any different.

I sip my glass of ice cold water, allowing the chill to run through me as I swallow my mouthful. The coldness is welcome, and currently matches my heart. No warmth circulates within me. Sean is prattling on about how he envisions the meeting going and I am half listening, until I see Monica stride through the front doors. I instantly scowl at her. I hate this woman with a passion. She sashays her way to our table, being led by a waitress, her smirk pissing me off.

"Good afternoon," she says, smugness rife within her tone. Sean stands up and shakes Monica's hand. Her eyes roam over Sean and I know that she is sizing him up now that she has had her way with Ben. My Ben. This woman oozes cougar-like qualities and I can't quite believe that her husband is oblivious to her slutty nature. "Hello Kayleigh," she says distracting me from my thoughts, her hand held out to me. I want to recoil from her, get as far away as possible, but I can't do that. If we lose this contract because of me, then my head will be on the chopping block for sure.

"Monica," I say in a sickly sweet tone as I take her hand in a vice like grip. I momentarily witness her smirk falter, but she quickly regains herself, shaking my hand and then letting go as soon as possible. I appear to have the upper hand as I sense her uncomfortableness. That upper hand doesn't last long as she sits down and reveals someone stood behind her. My mouth drops open, my eyes go wide as I take in the sight of Ben standing there. He has the decency to cast his eyes downwards, refusing to look at me.

Oh, so this is her game plan. Shake you up by bringing your ex with her. Your ex who she has fucked. Don't give her the satisfaction of crumbling Kayleigh, it's what she wants. Make the bitch pay. Make the bitch suffer.

Ben sits down, looking awkward and Monica slides up next to him, making sure that there isn't an inch of space between them.

"So," she starts, her leg rubbing against Ben's. "Shall we order some food before we get started?"

"Actually, I think that we should just get straight down to business," Sean says, making Monica reel back in shock. I look to him and see that his jaw is set into a firm line, his teeth clearly clenched together. I want to ask him what he is doing, I want to ask him why he has just jeopardised this meeting by being blunt, but I can't. I will have to wait until we are on our own before he can answer my questions. It would look highly unprofessional for me to question his strategy in front of potential clients.

"Oh, right, of course," Monica replies, flabbergasted. "Let me introduce you to Ben first," she says, placing her arm around his shoulders. He visibly

152

freezes in place, his eyes quickly darting to mine before they look down again. "Ben is going to be coming on board with me. I need someone to run things whilst I make vital decisions, and Ben is the perfect choice."

"Nice to meet you," Sean says, although he doesn't look like he means it. Sean would know who Ben is. Ben turned up to my office occasionally, and I know that everyone was always shocked by it, seeing as I am a lost cause in most of their eyes. I remain silent.

Sean wastes no time in getting down to business, barely pausing for breath. I don't take in anything as I watch Monica and Ben together. Ben looks ashamed, Monica looks like the cat that got the cream. Ben doesn't talk, Monica takes the lead. Ben looks miserable, Monica looks elated. The stark contrast between the two shows me that things aren't as rosy as Monica would have me believe. I excuse myself to go to the bathroom. The walk feels long, each step causing me a ridiculous amount of effort to make. I reach the ladies but am stopped by someone placing their hand on my arm. I close my eyes from the touch. I know that touch intimately.

"Kayleigh?" Ben says softly, concern evident in his tone. I keep my eyes closed, teeth gritted. *Don't let him in Kayleigh. He fucked you over and didn't give you a second thought.*

"Kayleigh, please look at me?" I shake my head at him, not wanting him to be able to see the hurt in my eyes. I can't appear weak. I need to be in control.

"Let me go Ben," I say, my voice hard.

"No."

"I don't want to talk to you. We have nothing left to say to one another."

"I beg to differ." He scoffs at my response causing my anger to surge. I whirl around, ripping my arm out of his grip.

"I've told you that I want nothing more to do with you. Why can't you just leave me alone?"

"Because we're not done here!" he shouts at me, making me raise my eyes to look at him. There is a fire in him that I haven't seen for a long time. A determination. "You can't just shut me out Kayleigh. We need to talk."

"No, we don't."

"Yes we do!" Ben has stepped closer to me, his body is almost flush against mine. I can't back away as I find myself trapped between him and the wall.

"I'm not doing this now Ben. We are at a work meeting, what the hell is wrong with you?" Not to mention that we are in a fucking restaurant and anyone could hear us.

"When then Kayleigh? Because all you have done is ignore me."

"You cheated on me, what more is there to say?"

"How many times do I have to tell you? I didn't fucking cheat."

"No? So that woman sitting out there with us didn't have her lips attached to yours? Are you seriously trying to tell me that it was all just innocent? Do you expect me to believe your bullshit after she showed up at my house and told me that you were a good fuck?"

"She what?" Ben looks flabbergasted at what I have just said. If I were a fool then I would be inclined to believe that he knew nothing about her little visit to me, but I am no fool. Not anymore.

"Ben?"

"Huh, speak of the devil," I say as I see Monica come up behind us, her eyes taking in our close proximity.

"Is everything okay here?" she says as she walks forwards and places her hand on Ben's shoulder. I see him physically recoil from her touch and it fills me with a smugness to see her rejected by him.

"We're fine," Ben replies sharply.

"Um, I think our business is concluded here Ben. We really need to be getting back to the office now." Monica looks unsure of herself for the first time. My gaze returns to Ben and he is looking at me fiercely.

"We're not finished," he says to me quietly before walking away. Monica follows him, but when she glances back at me, I hit her with a smirk.

Good work Kayleigh. You stood your ground and pissed that bitch off in the process. The time is coming for her to realise that she never should have messed around with you in the first place.......

Chapter Thirty-Seven.

Sean and I are walking back to the office when he decides to bring up how the meeting went.

"So, that was a little awkward wasn't it?" he says, and I can feel him looking at me.

"How do you mean?" I have no desire to discuss my shitty love life with Sean.

"Oh come on, you're not seriously going to try and tell me that you were okay with that woman bringing your ex-partner into the mix?" I stop walking, and Sean follows suit.

"I don't really want to talk about it." I guess that Lacey couldn't keep her mouth shut and told Sean my private business. She must have because Sean had no reason to behave the way in which he did in the meeting otherwise.

"That's fine, but I just want you to know that Monica pulled a really shitty move today. We may not have ever really had much to say to each other, but just know that, I was firmly in your corner today." I feel tears spring to my eyes and I rapidly blink to try and make them disappear.

"Thank you," I reply, my voice fading and coming out as a whisper. Sean nods and we resume walking. "How did you know that Ben and I had broken up?"

"We work in an office Kayleigh, and there is nothing better than a bit of juicy gossip for most of the workers to get their teeth into."

"You mean, you have all been talking about me?"

"No. I just overheard a few things."

"Like what?" I knew that they spoke about me, but actually hearing Sean confirm it makes me feel even smaller than I already do.

"I'm just going to be blunt because that's how I roll."

"Okay." Now I feel even more nervous.

"Basically the Chinese whispers going around are that Ben realised that you are crazy and left, or that Ben cheated on you." I suck in a breath at his words.

"Wow, you really don't sugar coat things do you?"

"Nope. I find it best to be upfront, unless you are trying to schmooze a client." I continue to walk in a daze, his words echoing around my head. "I just want to say for the record that I don't think that you are crazy. I just think that you have had some shitty luck and people aren't willing to give you a chance, me included in that statement. But, I have seen how close you and Lacey have grown over the last few weeks, and I see a change in you. You appear warmer when she is around."

"Do I?" I am a little shocked at how observant he has been.

"Yeah. Lacey brings out the good in people, and she is doing that with you." Fucking hell, he really has been paying attention. And my acting skills around Lacey are better than I thought. I have managed to fool him as well as Lacey into thinking that I have opened up to her and become more likeable. My lips pull into a smile at the thought.

"She's a great person."

"She really is." His eyes take on a far off dreamy look and our conversation comes to a close. *Well, well, well, we are doing a fantastic job of fooling people aren't we? Sean is even beginning to warm to you. Fantastic. It will make our end goal all the more satisfactory. No one can touch us. We are the elite, and they are the pawns in our game. I told you that it would be easy. I told you that you had it in you to go through with it. You are a fighter*

157

Kayleigh, and with me by your side, we can take on the world.

Chapter Thirty-Eight.

"Hey guys," I say as I open the front door and invite Lacey and Sean inside.

"Hey," they both say in unison as they enter the hall way and take off their coats. I point to where they can hang them and then I lead them through to the kitchen.

"Take a seat at the table and I'll get us some drinks," I say, gesturing for them to sit down. It's been a few days since the horrendous meeting with Monica and Ben. I decided that I would invite Sean and Lacey round so that I could get more of an insight into how they act outside of work. Sean has been friendlier towards me, and Lacey was ecstatic when I extended the invite to the both of them. Obviously Sean and Lacey haven't been trying to hide their relationship at work anymore. It appears that everyone in the office knows that they are an item, so they have forgone the effort of hiding it.

Taking the drinks over to the table, I then grab the food that I have prepared and place it on the table so that we can all serve ourselves. I opted to make buffet food so that it gives a more relaxed feeling in the hope that they will feel comfortable enough to let me see what really happens between them.

"So Kayleigh," Sean says as he picks up a mini quiche and places it on his plate. "Have you heard from Ben at all since the other day?"

"Sean," Lacey scolds him, nudging him in his side with her elbow.

"Ow, what did you do that for?" he says, rubbing his side and giving Lacey a questioning look.

"You can't just ask personal stuff like that. Don't you know anything about women?" Lacey raises one eyebrow at him and he continues to look perplexed.

"It's okay," I say intervening so that the atmosphere doesn't become tense.

"No it's not," Lacey responds, not backing down.

"We're all friends here, I don't mind Sean asking me. Honestly," I say, plastering a big grin on my face. *She's going to ruin everything if she doesn't shut her face.*

"See?" Sean says, but this still earns him a scowl from Lacey.

"In answer to your question Sean," I say, steering the conversation away from them having an argument, "I haven't heard anything, which I am grateful for. The last thing that I want to do is hear his lies." Sean knows that Ben cheated, I told him the other day and I think it has gone a long way to gaining his trust. I'm still uncertain whether Lacey told him anything or not, but I haven't asked the question because I don't want to rock the boat. I need to keep my focus. Nothing can hinder my plan.

"Honestly Kay, I don't know how you managed to keep your cool at the meeting. I would have gone mad had it been me sat there," Lacey says taking a sip of her wine. I stop myself from cringing at the way she calls me Kay. It seems to be a new habit that she has picked up and I hate it, but I don't want to say anything that may make her think twice about me, so I keep my mouth shut.

"Oh really?" Sean says, waggling his eyebrows at her. *Here we go, you're about to witness an insight. Pay close attention Kayleigh, you don't want to miss anything.* I adhere to the voice's advice and I just watch as they have a little conversation between themselves. They are flirting outrageously and Lacey has a constant smile on her face. Watching them interact makes my heart pang. They seem to have such an easy flow of banter between them. I always had to work hard at the banter. I always had to keep the voice at bay, ignoring the snide remarks. A part of me used to feel exhausted by it, but now that the voice can speak freely, I feel more energised. Almost as if the voice gives me a purpose, a reason to continue down the path that I am creating. A knock at the front door has me standing to my feet and excusing myself from their sickly display of lust, or love, I don't care to work out which one it is. I exit the kitchen and walk down the hall way, feeling ticked off that I am being interrupted during vital research. As I fling the door open, I gasp at the person standing there.

"Hi," he says, as if I should be expecting him. I fold my arms across my chest in defence.

"Ben." There is no warmth in my voice.

"I was wondering if we could have that chat now?" I scoff at him. He really doesn't think that I have anything better to do than sit around waiting for him?

"Now's not a good time. I have company." With that, Sean laughs loudly and I can see Ben's eyes narrow as he hears the sound of another male in the house.

"Who's that?" he asks, trying to peer around me. I quickly unfold my arms and pull the door closed behind me.

"It's none of your business."

"Is that another guy in there?"

"Wow, top marks for Ben," I reply sarcastically.

"Are you seeing someone else?" His voice cracks a little as he asks the question. *Oh Kayleigh, this is brilliant. With Ben's perfect timing, you can really stir the pot.*

"I don't have to explain myself to you. You lost the right to ask me anything from the moment that you let that woman stick her tongue in your mouth."

"I've already told you that I didn't cheat."

"And I've told you that I have no desire to hear the bullshit that you want to spin my way." I remain defiant, enjoying the look of panic on his face.

"Please Kayleigh, please just talk to me." He's pleading and it brings me immense satisfaction that he is having to work to gain my attention. I have never really had the upper hand before, and now that I have, I am going to bask in every second of it.

"I can't promise anything. As you can see, my free time is not quite so free anymore." I don't wait for an answer as I walk back into the house, shutting the door on Ben who looks like he has seen a ghost. I let out a little chuckle as I make my way back to the kitchen. *Well, well, it seems that the learner has become the master. You played that beautifully. I enjoyed being able to sit back and relax as you made Ben sweat. Now you just have to up your game with the two idiots in the kitchen, and then the fun really begins.*

Chapter Thirty-Nine.

"Kayleigh?" Mr Harvey barks down the phone at me.

"Yes sir?" I answer like an obedient little dog.

"My office, *now.*" The phone goes dead and I gulp. Being summoned to Mr Harvey's office fills me with dread. The last two times that I was summoned in there, it was for reasons that catastrophically changed my life. The first time to be introduced to Lacey, and the second to be told about the client meeting with Sean, which turned out to be the worst of the two.

Lacey. She really is stupid.

I ignore the voice and stand on wobbly legs, making my way out of my office and towards whatever problem Mr Harvey is going to chuck my way. I can't let the voice distract me right now. Facing Mr Harvey, I need my wits about me.

"Where are you off to?" Sean says, coming up behind me and falling into step as I continue to walk.

"I've been called to see Mr Harvey."

"Oh shit."

"I know." Everyone knows that being called there isn't good. I can only hope that Mr Harvey is having an off day and has decided to call me in here for something good. I stop outside his office door and stare at the handle as if it is going to bite me.

"Well, good luck. Whatever he wants, you're going to need it."

"Thanks Sean." Sean gives me a smile as he walks off and I take a deep breath. I knock on the door and hear Mr Harvey's sharp tone as he yells for me to 'come in.' I do so and quickly shut the door behind me upon entering. I keep my eyes trained on the floor, waiting for him to invite me to sit down.

"Kayleigh, take a seat." At this I look up and am almost floored by the person that I see sitting on one of the chairs.

"Monica?" I say, my voice quiet as I begin to get a bad feeling settling in the pit of my stomach.

"Just sit down," Mr Harvey says. Monica is smirking, her back poker straight, one of her legs crossed over the other conveniently showing an ample amount of flesh. I walk to the chair next to her and I fight the urge to move it away from her. I need to remain professional. I avert my eyes to look at Mr Harvey, and his face is like thunder. His cheeks are a little rosy and his brows are pinched into a frown.

"Kayleigh, I sent you with Sean the other day to speak to Monica and her colleague." I nod at him, not daring to utter a sound until it is necessary to do so. "I understand that meeting didn't end particularly well."

"Ummmm…."

"Don't mumble at me," he says, his cheeks reddening some more. "Just explain to me in your words what happened." I gulp loudly, and I am positive that they must be able to hear it. The tension is radiating around the room and I want nothing more than to just get out of here.

"Well, we attended the meeting, but I am unsure how it ended as I went to the ladies' room." Even I can hear the wobble in my voice. *Pull it together and make yourself sound confident. Don't crumble just because that bitch is sat there.*

"Are you sure about that?" Mr Harvey says.

"Yes sir," I reply with a nod of my head. I feel like a naughty school kid getting told off by the head teacher.

"Monica," Mr Harvey says turning his attention away from me. "Would you care to reiterate what you told me before I called Kayleigh in here?"

"Of course." Monica turns her body so that it is angled towards me, her smug face making me want to slap her. "Kayleigh," she starts, placing her hand on my arm briefly. I can't help the sudden movement as I pull my arm away from her as if she has burned my skin. "Mr Harvey has explained to me your job role within this company, and he has also told me that you don't usually accompany others on meetings to clients." I already feel demoralised by this woman and she has only just started. "I thought it was best that I brought something to Mr Harvey's attention." She pauses for effect, making it look like this is difficult for her. I grit my teeth together so that I don't say anything to make this situation worse. "I just, I don't think that it is appropriate for you to be meeting with others after the things you said to me outside of the ladies' room."

"What?" I say before I can stop myself. What the hell is she talking about?

"I.... I really wish that things could have ended differently but when you called me a cheap slut, I felt that I needed to bring this to your boss's attention." My mouth drops open in response. "I have to say that your words hurt me Kayleigh just when I was starting to believe that we were going to have a beautiful working relationship." Monica feigns getting upset by getting a tissue out of her handbag, which is on the floor beside her, and starts to dab underneath her eyes.

"It's okay, take your time," Mr Harvey says, a soft smile forming on his lips.

"Thank you. It's just so hard to come here and put someone's job in jeopardy."

"Are you being serious right now?" I say, my voice high.

"I don't think now is the time to be saying anything," Mr Harvey says, his tone back to its stern manner as he stares daggers at me.

"Oh gosh, I feel awful about this, but I had no idea that bringing Ben with me was going to elicit such a strong reaction in you. I honestly didn't mean to cause you any hurt Kayleigh. I just, I can't bear the thought of working with a company who has made me feel so worthless. I mean, as if calling me a slut wasn't bad enough, the fact that you then started to comment on my clothing choice was unbearable."

"This is all lies….."

"I mean, I like to dress nice but to be called 'mutton dressed as lamb' was uncalled for."

"You bitch," the insult slips out before I can stop it.

"Kayleigh, that is quite enough," Mr Harvey interjects. "I will not have clients spoken to like that. Apologise now." His voice is loud but it's not as loud as the pounding in my ears. He has fallen for her story hook, line and sinker. Not only has she taken my man, but now she is going after my job.

"Oh please, I don't want to cause anymore fuss," Monica says with a wave of her hand.

"Why are you doing this?" I ask her, ignoring my boss.

"Doing what?" the innocence in her voice must have took her years to perfect.

"Trying to ruin my life."

"I am doing no such thing," she says, aghast. "Mr Harvey, please, can we just end this now. I don't feel comfortable being in here with her."

"Of course. Kayleigh, go to your office. I will speak to you later." His instant dismissal of me makes me mad. A surge of anger rises up within me, and I can no longer hold it in. I can no longer let these people treat me as if I am nothing but a pawn in their pathetic games. It's time that I stood up to them. I have been bullied all my life, and I refuse to let it happen anymore.

"No."

"No?" Mr Harvey says, outraged that I am speaking back to him.

"That's right. I'm not going anywhere."

"Oh goodness, I didn't mean to cause all of this trouble," Monica says and I turn my steely gaze on her.

"Your middle name is trouble. You have been trying to fuck my life up since the moment that you entered it."

"This is preposterous," she exclaims, but I don't let her say anymore. It's my time to speak.

"You weren't content enough to take Ben away from me, so you thought you would come here and stir up some shit with my boss. What the hell did I ever do to you Monica? Why on earth did you take such a dislike to me?" The room remains silent, Mr Harvey wide-eyed and Monica continuing her damsel in distress act.

"I honestly don't know what you mean. I am a happily married woman….."

"Pah. Happily married my ass!"

"That's enough," Mr Harvey says rising to his feet. I follow his stance and stand tall. I will not be made to feel beneath him.

"I'm not FINISHED!" I shout, causing him to flop back down in his chair, his face suddenly going pale. "This woman," I say pointing to Monica, "has come in here and told you a pack of lies, but you would rather believe her word over mine. You would rather believe that I have done wrong instead of fighting my corner. I have done nothing but be a dutiful employee since I started working here. I have always done anything that has been asked of me, even if I didn't want to do it. I have never argued, and I have always kept myself to myself so that I didn't get caught up in the office politics in this place, but it has never been good enough. You have had it in for me too," I say, now pointing at Mr Harvey.

"I can assure you Kayleigh, I have never had a bad word to say about….."

"Bullshit," I cut him off, not wanting to hear his crap for another second longer. "You have belittled me, made me feel useless, made me feel like I am easily replaced. You employed Lacey without even consulting me, even though it was about my workload." My breathing is loud and laboured but I have more to say. "You have been dying to get rid of me, and this evil woman has given you a reason, even though she has lied."

"I'm not lying," Monica pipes up, her voice hurting my ears. I turn my body towards her and bend down slowly, until I am eye level with her. I see her gulp and I allow a smile to form in response. She didn't expect the meeting to take this path. She expected to see me humiliated, but instead I am calling her out.

"Don't fucking sit there and act like you are a saint. You are a vile, nasty piece of work, and I wish that I had never met you."

"I'm calling security," Mr Harvey says as he reaches for the phone.

"No need," I respond, my eyes still fixed on Monica. "I'm leaving." Before I stand up, I put my lips by Monica's ear and whisper so that only she can hear me, "you're going to regret the day that you ever fucked with me, just you wait and see." I stand and turn, putting my back to the both of them. As I reach the door, placing my hand on the handle, I turn back to look at Mr Harvey, deciding that I will save him the trouble of having to fire me. I say two simple words that sound so satisfying as they come out of my mouth.

"I quit."

Chapter Forty.

Fuck.

What have I done?

The reality of quitting my job is only just hitting me. I may have been full of confidence when I was in Mr Harvey's office but now, as I walk home, I feel like I have made a really bad choice. I saw red and instead of grovelling and begging to keep my job, I just quit. Just like that. No warning, I just did it.

You did the right thing Kayleigh. You refused to be treated like shit a moment longer. You took control. I'm so proud of you for standing up for yourself. You have no idea how long I have been waiting to see you blossom and believe me, you are blossoming. I laugh in response to the voice.

You see Kayleigh, you have gone through life letting others determine your path. You became a recluse, a nothing, a ball of human flesh that had nothing going on inside. But now, now you are holding your own. You have fucked off Ben, and now you have jacked your meaningless job. Things are going to go right for you from now. Just stick to the plan.....

"Oh yes, the plan, how could I forget," I say sarcastically. A couple walking past me give me a funny look, but I choose not to say anything. Why bother? Who ultimately cares about the crazy woman walking down the road talking to herself? No one. That's who, absolutely fucking no one.

I care.

I'm almost starting to think that the voice cares too much.....

Chapter Forty-One.

"I just thought that I would pop round and see if you were okay?" Lacey says as she stands on my doorstep with a bunch of flowers in her hand.

"I'm fine, why wouldn't I be?" I shrug my shoulders and invite her in. My only focus now is on making her pay. If she hadn't have showed up in the office, then maybe my job would have been more secure. Maybe I wouldn't have felt the need to quit. If Lacey hadn't been sharing my job role, then I would have been indispensable. Bitch.

"Well, you are the talk of the office," Lacey exclaims, a little excitement in her voice.

"Tea?" I ignore her comment. I don't wish to discuss my outburst.

"No thank you, I can't stay long. Sean is taking me out for a meal." With my back to her I roll my eyes.

"Sounds nice." Sounds boring more like. *Make yourself sound happier, will you? You don't want her to start questioning your friendship.* I turn around and the smile has dropped from Lacey's face. She looks concerned. "I'm sorry," I start, putting my acting skills to the test once again. "I didn't mean to sound so miserable. I guess that, I'm just a little shocked at how today has played out. I didn't go into work this morning expecting to quit my job."

"From what I heard, that Monica woman is a nasty piece of work."

"Oh?" My interest is piqued at the mention of Monica.

"Rumour has it that she is busy keeping Mr Harvey sweet, if you know what I mean?" she winks at me, leaving no room for me to doubt her meaning at all. *Oh, so that's why he didn't even try and hear me out, because he is also fucking Monica.*

171

"Seriously?"

"Uh huh. Karen in marketing saw them and was sworn to secrecy. Of course she hasn't kept quiet about it, so I doubt it will be long before she is disposed of." Lacey speaks so flippantly, as if this isn't a big deal. *To her it isn't. But to us, it's ammo.*

"Wow."

"Are you sure you're okay?"

"Yes. Actually, I think that this could be really good for me. I haven't been happy there for a while, so it will give me a chance to concentrate on new ventures." Little does she know that my new ventures include her as the main character. Sucker.

"Got anything in mind?"

"Not anything specific." Best to keep her in the dark. Don't want her catching on to anything.

"Well, if there is anything that I can help you with, just ask."

"Sure." *Ha, as if.*

"I'm glad I met you Kayleigh. I think of you as a close friend now, so please don't let you leaving hinder our friendship." She looks so genuine that I almost laugh in her face. She has no idea of the fate that I have in mind for her.

"Trust me Lacey, nothing is going to come between us."

Chapter Forty-Two.
One week later.

18:45.

It's time.

No more waiting around.

It's now or never........

Chapter Forty-Three.

19:26.

There she is, walking to her car like her shit doesn't stink.

Keep your eye on her.

Don't let her get away.

I watch as Monica gets into her car, oblivious to the fact that I am in the car behind her, waiting to follow her, to put my plan into action. She has caused me so much pain and after tonight, she will be the one that is suffering, not me.

Chapter Forty-Four.

19:47.

Monica pulls onto the drive way of the house that she shares with her husband. I can see him coming out of the front door as I stop opposite their drive way. His lips are moving, and I open my car window so that I can try and hear what he is saying.

"What time do you call this?" he shouts, clearly pissed off that she hasn't come home sooner. I don't hear her response and I can't judge her reaction as her back is to me.

"For fuck sake Monica, why can't you just stick to your word?" he huffs and puffs his way to a brand new Mercedes, getting into the car and pulling off of the drive way. Monica turns and watches him screech down the road, her eyes look sad. Her demeanour screams that of a down-trodden woman. Most people would have sympathy for her, but not me. She has destroyed my life, and now she will pay. Monica turns her back to me once more, and that is when I make my move. Quickly getting out of my car, I run across the road and am behind her within seconds, the gun in my pocket digging into my thigh. Before she has time to register what is happening, I push her, making her fall flat on her face. She lets out a loud shriek as her cheek collides with the gravel on the floor. My eyes dart all around to see if anyone has just witnessed me shoving her to the ground. There is no one.

Good girl. Now get her inside the house. Quick. Monica turns onto her back, spluttering.

"Get up," I say in my most aggressive voice.

"Kayleigh?" she seems slightly confused by my appearance here, but it won't take me too long to rectify her confusion.

"I said get up."

"What the hell are you doing?"

"All will become clear in the next few minutes Monica. Now get the fuck up and get inside the house." She laughs. She actually fucking laughs at me.

"I'm sorry but, have I stepped onto a really bad film set?" she says through her laughter. My anger rises with every word that she speaks. *She's not taking you seriously Kayleigh. Go in for the kill.* With my adrenaline at an all-time high, I move my hand and put it in my pocket, feeling the cold metal of the gun against my fingers. I do another quick check around to see if anyone has appeared on the street, but it is empty. With my nerves threatening to make me chicken out of my plan, I quickly pull the gun out and point it towards Monica. Her laughter stops. The colour drains from her face. Her eyes go wide. Her mouth falls open.

"Do you think you're on a film set now?" I sneer at her. I don't want to stand out here too long with a gun in my hand. The more time it takes to get her in the house, the more chance there is of someone seeing and calling the police on me. "Get in the house." I pronounce each word slowly so that she understands my urgency.

"Okay," she whispers as she clambers to her feet and turns to walk up the path. I follow her, keeping the gun trained on her just in case she decides to do something stupid like trying to get the gun off of me. We both walk in silence, and I let the tension build.

Once you're inside, you can enjoy what is to unfold.

Chapter Forty-Five.

20:14.

Huh, I figured that it was later than that. It felt like forever stood outside trying to get Monica to enter the bloody house. She now sits in front of me, on her plush white sofa, looking petrified. Good. Serves her right. Fucking bitch.

"So, Monica, what time is your husband coming back home?" I ask. I'm hoping that she will be truthful and that I won't have to spend ages coaxing the answer out of her.

"Um, he's just nipped to the shop." *She's lying.* I guess the answer isn't going to be straightforward then. The gun is still in my hand, my arm hanging down by my side.

"Oh Monica, I thought that having my little friend with me would mean that you would cut the bullshit, but I guess I was wrong." I hold the gun up and tap it lightly with my other finger. Monica's eyes fill with tears, but it doesn't do anything to make me soften towards her. This woman is evil. And evil must be punished.

"I…… I'm not lying….."

"Don't insult me."

"I'm not trying to….."

"Just tell me what time he is coming home." She's still watching the gun. Her body shaking.

"I don't know," she responds, quietly.

"Speak up, I didn't quite catch that." My voice is loud and appears to echo around the large room.

"I don't know," she repeats, a fraction louder than last time.

"Where has he gone?"

"To a business meeting."

"So that means we could be alone for a while then?"

"I...... I guess so." *Or the meeting could have gone tits up and he's on his way back here right now. Get a move on with what you came here to do and stop pussy footing around.*

"Right. Now, I need you to answer some questions for me, do you think that you can do that?" Monica nods her head as a few tears escape her eyes and fall down her cheeks. "Good. Question number one, why do you hate me?"

"I don't hate you."

"DON'T FUCKING LIE TO ME!" I raise the gun pointing it at her. She puts her hands in front of her face and lets out a high-pitched squeal which makes the hairs on my body stand to attention.

"Please don't hurt me."

"I'm hoping that it won't come to that, but if you continue to lie to me and piss me off, then I will have no choice but to blow your brains out. Understand?" Monica nods her head again and lowers her hands. "Why do you hate me?" I keep the gun pointing at her. I'm quite enjoying watching how terrified she is.

"I never hated you Kayleigh, I was jealous of you."

"Jealous?" This answer has completely thrown me. Why the hell would she be jealous of me? "Why?"

"Because, you're young, Ben adored you, and I wanted him." She closes her eyes and takes a few breaths. I wait patiently, needing to hear the rest of her answer. "I had always had a bit of a thing for Ben, and he kept refusing me. I've been married to my husband for a long time, but the love died years ago. Our marriage is for convenience. When I saw how Ben looked at you, I wanted that for myself. I wanted to be made to feel special, to feel loved and wanted."

"So you thought that you would ruin my happiness? Did it make you feel better about yourself?" I actually believe what she is telling me, but I can't feel sorry for her. She stole something that was mine.

"For a short while it did." She looks to the floor and hangs her head.

"So once you fucked Ben, why didn't you just leave me alone?"

"I didn't fuck Ben," she says with a sigh.

"What?" her words have floored me. She has to be lying again. She told me that he was a good fuck.

"I didn't sleep with him." She looks up, her face full of shame. It's a look that I have never seen on her before. It's a little unnerving. "He turned me down, even after you kicked him out."

"But I saw you both kissing."

"He pulled away from me."

"No. No. No." This can't be happening. She can't be telling the truth.

She's played you Kayleigh. She's played you like a fool, and you were unable to see it.

"YOU COULDN'T SEE IT EITHER!" I shout, making Monica jump with fright. "YOU TOLD ME THAT BEN WAS CHEATING!"

"Who are you talking to?" Monica asks, but I ignore her. I need the voice to answer me.

He would have done one day, I just made you see sense sooner.

"Oh my god," I say, my body shaking with rage.

I was doing it for you. For your own good. The doubt was already in your mind. I just made it stronger.

179

"Ben was telling me the truth all along. He never cheated."

"No, he didn't," Monica answers, unaware that I wasn't actually talking to her.

"Shut up," I tell her. Her mouth closes quickly, her lips pursed together.

I warned you about letting others into our life together. I warned you of the danger in letting someone into your heart, but you ignored me. On the day that you met Ben, I told you to stay away. I told you that I would look after you, but you didn't listen. My mind flashes back to the day that Ben and I bumped into one another. He took me for a drink, the voice tried to worm its way in, but I liked Ben too much to let it take over. The voice didn't like that and now, here I am, being played yet again.

"Kayleigh?" Monica says, her voice wavering.

"What?"

"Please, can we just call a truce?"

"A truce? You want a fucking truce? After everything that you have done to me, you want to be the one to make amends?"

"Yes, please."

"You lied to me, took Ben away, and then you came after my job. You really think that I am just going to be happy with a few words of friendliness from you?"

"I……. I……. Please…….. Please don't do anything stupid."

"I have thought every aspect of this through Monica. I didn't just get a gun on a whim and decide to come round here, give me some fucking credit."

"Okay, I'm sorry, I just…… maybe we could get you some help?" I freeze for a second at her words. Help? She thinks that I need help?

"Help for what? What makes you think that I need help?"

"Well, um, maybe the fact that you are stood in my lounge with a gun in your hand."

"Oh wow, you really are a piece of work aren't you?"

"No, I just want to help you."

"No you don't. You tried to ruin me. You tried to destroy me, but you didn't bank on me becoming stronger. You didn't bank on me turning up here to call you out."

"I'm sorry," she says, crying harder now. "I'm so sorry. I don't know what else to say." I watch her as she sobs, her whole body trembling violently. Sympathy evades me. Anger engulfs me. Rage overpowers me. I've lost Ben. I've lost my job. I've nothing left to fight for.

"I just wanted you to leave me alone, but you couldn't do it. So, your apologies mean nothing. Your tears mean nothing. You need to pay for what you have done." I click the safety off of the gun and adjust it so that it is pointing straight at her face.

"Kayleigh," she says in a panicked voice. "Don't do this."

"Do what? What do you think I am going to do?" He erratic breathing reaches my ears and my adrenaline surges once again from the feeling of power that I have over this woman. Power that I am unwilling to let go of.

"Please don't shoot me." I cackle, loudly, manically. The sound of her begging is sweet, but the sound of her dying is going to be even sweeter.

"I wish that I could forgive you. I wish that I was the type of person to let go of the grudges that I hold, but I'm not. The pain that you have caused me is indescribable, so I hope that it was worth it."

"You really are crazy." It's the last words I hear from her before I pull the trigger. The sound of the gun rings out and within seconds I watch as the bullet buries itself in Monica's head. Her eyes go dead, her body goes limp, and blood slowly starts to seep from the bullet hole between her eyes. I watch it trickle down her face, a weight lifting off of my shoulders.

You did it Kayleigh. You took charge and you did it.
"Yes I did."
I'm proud of you.
"And I'm pissed at you."
I know, but in time you will come to see that I have only done what is best for you. In time you will forgive me. I am always here. I'm not going anywhere. I am your strength. Without me, you would never have made this plan, and then you would never have regained your power. Now, we can discuss this more later, but right now, you need to continue with the plan. Get moving Kayleigh, there is more work to be done.

Chapter Forty-Six.

21:12.

I have driven to Mr Harvey's house. I watch through the window and see that he is sat with his wife, at the kitchen table, sipping wine. His wife is talking and he looks bored shitless. This part of the plan won't take long, and this is where I need to time it just right because once I go through with this, I won't have much time to get to the next place. Mr Harvey made my working life a misery. His arrogant manner has grated on me one too many times. I allow my mind to flash back to all of the times that he reprimanded me. All of the embarrassment that he caused me in front of others. The way in which he was so quick to disregard anything that I said to him. And the total lack of respect for his wife just adds to his crappy personality. He has cheated on her, and she is unaware. After the pain that I experienced at thinking that Ben had betrayed me, it is my job to make sure that another woman doesn't experience that hurt. Mr Harvey will never change, and I need to make him stop. It's my duty. I go to the front door and knock hard. The gun is in my back pocket. I place my hand on the butt of the gun and wait for the door to open. A few seconds go past before the door swings open and Mr Harvey's chubby face appears.

"Kayleigh?" he says, shocked to see me here.

"Good evening Mr Harvey."

"What are you doing here?"

"Who is it?" I hear his wife shout from another room.

"Well, I thought that I would come and put your wife out of her misery of being married to you." Before he can reply, I pull the gun out on him and fire. The bullet lodges in his chest and he collapses to his knees. He splutters and falls onto his side as his wife comes into view. She screams and throws herself down beside him.

"Trust me Mrs Harvey, you're going to thank me for that one day."

"Oh my god, you shot him!" her voice is verging on hysterical. Can't say I blame her, but I think she needs to know what a sleaze she is married to.

"Mrs Harvey, he has been cheating on you with a woman named Monica. He has no morals. To put I bluntly, he's an asshole. Plain and simple. You will be better off without him." I don't wait for a response. I need to move quickly. I walk back to my car and get in.

Nice work. Now for the next part……..

Chapter Forty-Seven.

21:48.

Quick Kayleigh. No time to waste.

"I'm going as fast as I can," I say, exasperated at the voice getting annoyed that I haven't been quick enough.

It's not good enough. Do you want to be caught?

"Of course not."

Then fucking hurry up.

I rush out of the car and knock on Lacey's door, pounding hard. My heart is racing, my adrenaline is pumping. I fidget as I wait for her to answer the door. When two minutes have gone by and there is still no response, I start to panic. She didn't say that she was going out tonight, so why isn't she answering? I knock again, even harder than before. Another two minutes and still nothing.

"Bollocks," I say out loud, pulling my mobile phone from my pocket. I find Lacey's number and call her. As the phone rings I become more agitated. If I can't find her, then all of my work goes to shit.

"Hello?" she says on the fourth ring.

"Oh thank god for that. Where are you?" I say, I don't have time for small talk.

"Kayleigh?"

"Yeah, it's me." Shouldn't she know that already? My number is in her phone so it's fucking obvious that it's me. "I need to see you, where are you?"

"Oh. I'm at The Kingston. Do you need me to come home?" I do a quick calculation and realise that The Kingston is fifteen minutes away. That's too long. I can't just sit here and wait for her to come back.

"I'm at your place now so, is there any chance that you could meet me half way? There's a car park about five minutes from where you are, you know, on Main street. I can be there in a few minutes if I hurry."

"Course I can. Is everything okay?"

"I'll explain when I get there. Thanks Lacey."

"No problem. See you soon." I hang up the phone and get back into my car. I quickly fire up the engine and tear down the road in the direction that I need. Trust Lacey to go and put a curveball into my plans.

Chapter Forty-Eight.

22:00.

I pull into the car park and see Lacey stood in the far corner, and she isn't alone.

"Fuck." Sean is beside her, his arm around her shoulders. I should have realised that he would be with her. I park the car in front of them and get out, already planning how to get rid of him.

"Hi guys," I say, breathlessly.

"Hi," Sean says.

"What's wrong?" Lacey asks me as she steps forward.

"I, um......" *Get rid of him Kayleigh. The plan won't work if he is stood there.* "I......"

"What is it?" she asks in a gentle voice, her hand resting on my arm. "Jesus Kayleigh, you're shaking like a leaf." My body is clearly going into shock from all that has happened tonight, but I need to block it out. I need to see this through.

"I can't tell you with Sean here," I whisper, hoping that she will take the bait and get rid of him.

"Oh. Okay, give me a sec." She turns away from me and speaks to Sean in hushed whispers. I watch out of the corner of my eye, praying that he won't question my need to be alone with her. He shouldn't do seeing as we're 'friends' but in the event that he won't go away, I will just have to carry out the plan with him here. It just won't go the way that I wanted it to, but I will have to improvise. The seconds are ticking by and I know that I am running out of time. I tap my foot lightly on the ground. I prick my ears for the sound of any sirens in the distance, but there is nothing. Just the faint sound of cars travelling along the main road.

"So, what's up?" she says coming back to stand in front of me, Sean having disappeared.

"Where's Sean gone?" I need to make sure that he's not too close.

"He's walking back to the pub. I said that I would ask you to drop me there when we're done instead of me walking by myself."

"Oh, sure."

"So come on, tell me what's bothering you."

"Well, it's uh, I don't quite know how to....."

"Kayleigh?" she says, placing her hand on my shoulder.

"Get off me." My voice is low, but there is plenty of warning laced there. Lacey looks momentarily shocked by my reaction.

"Hey, it's okay. It's just me Kay."

"No," I say, shaking my head at her. "Don't do that. Don't come across all nicey nice."

"What?" She looks genuinely confused. I'm not fooled. Another act by her. Another way to try and make herself look innocent.

"You know, I really didn't think that you would be dumb enough to stick by me for this long, but you proved me wrong Lacey."

"Proved you wrong?" Her eyebrows are drawn together as I watch her trying to figure out my words.

"Yep. You are a tougher woman than I gave you credit for." Lacey allows a small smile to cross her face at this, but the smile won't last for long. She thinks that I am being kind, but she is about to get the wake-up call of her life. "You have been kind to me, befriended me, and included me. If I were anyone else then they would be thanking their lucky stars to have a friend like you. Unfortunately, I'm not anyone else. I'm me, and I have

188

seen through your act since day one." My face hardens, hers becomes surprised.

"Um, I'm sorry, what?"

"You heard me. The act that you put on is good I'll give you that, but don't you find it draining? Don't you get sick of the sound of your own sickly-sweet voice?" I mimic her voice for effect.

"I, I don't understand. What is happening here?" Her voice is firm, but there is a definite wobble there. She's nervous, and she certainly has every right to be.

"Things haven't exactly gone to the plan, so I'm going to have to do a shorter version of this instead."

"Of what?" Lacey starts to back away from me as I move towards her. "Kay, please, tell me what's wrong."

"Don't fucking call me that. My name is Kayleigh, not Kay." She keeps backing up until she can go no further. Her back hits a wall and with me in front of her, she's trapped. A large tree stands to the right of us, it's branches hanging over, the leaves giving us a little bit of shelter. Unless you come in from the left of the car park, you would never know that we were here. "Do you know how long I have wanted to tell you what I really think about you?" She shakes her head in response, her lips remaining shut. "Months. Fucking months of hearing your whiny voice has almost driven me mad. Almost."

"I don't understand, I thought that we were friends?" she whispers.

"I know," I reply with a chuckle. "I did a great job of making you think that we had become close, don't you think?" She doesn't respond as she awaits my next move. "Well, in keeping with the short version, this is the part where I tell you how much I hate you. I despise you Lacey. You came into my life and helped to destroy it. You are just as bad as everyone else. Thinking you're so fucking perfect. Acting like a fucking angel at every opportunity."

"Why are you saying these things? Why are you being so mean?"

"Mean? You think this is mean? Oh princess, you ain't seen nothing yet......"

Chapter Forty-Nine.

22:21.

The gun is trained on Lacey.

My hand is shaking.

Tears are streaming down her face.

I can feel people stood behind us, watching the horror that is unfolding.

I click the safety off and place my finger over the trigger.

Sean has returned and is shouting at me.

I block him out.

I block everything out.

Nothing exists in this moment except for Lacey, myself and the voice.

Pull the trigger Kayleigh.

Set yourself free.

End your misery.

Take back control.

Flashbacks of my life surface. Mum shouting at me. Mum hitting me. Dad leaving me. Mum drinking. Mum telling me how pathetic I am. Ben stood before me. Ben making love to me. Ben with Monica. Monica taunting me. Monica ruining me. Mr Harvey reprimanding me. Lacey befriending me. Sean befriending me. Me duping them.

"Please Kayleigh. I'm your friend, you don't have to do this." Lacey's desperation is breaking through the fog that surrounds me.

"LACEY!" Sean shouts, urgency lacing his tone.

"Come on Kayleigh, you don't need to do this. It doesn't have to be this way," Lacey pleads.

Ignore her.

Pull the trigger.

End her life.

Better yours.
Control.
It's all about control.
You have the power, don't let go of it.

"Shut up. Just all of you shut up," I shout, needing them to give me a moment. There are too many thoughts, too many voices. It's hard to decipher each one as they merge into a whirlpool of noise.

"Give me the gun," Lacey says, her hand reaching out to me. I step back, the gun still trained on her. My finger ready to pull the trigger and end it all. All of my suffering. All of my pain could be gone within a second. All of my suffering could be banished forever.

Do it.
Do it now before it's too late.
Quickly.
Finish the plan.
Think of the plan.
Set yourself free.

'Kayleigh, please just listen to me,' a new voice says causing me panic. "You don't have to so this sweetheart."

"Dad?" I say, my voice a whisper, my bottom lip trembling with the sound of his voice after so long.

'Yeah, it's me.' I take a quick look around, but I don't see him.

"Where are you?" I ask, desperately wanting to see his face.

'I'm right here, deep inside of you. I always have been.'
Of course he's not actually here you stupid woman. He left you. He doesn't care about you.

"Stop," I say, confusion clouding my path. "Just stop." My left hand goes to my head as it pounds, making me wince. My right hand still holds the gun that points at Lacey.

'This isn't the way forward Kayleigh,' Dad says.

Don't listen to him. He just wants to hold you back and make you give control to him. Don't do it. Don't let him get the better of you. You have me, that's all you need. The voice becomes more urgent, sensing that it is losing its hold over me. My Dad's voice has overpowered it.

'I will look after you now. There's no need to be scared anymore. I'm sorry that I left you. I'm sorry that I wasn't around whilst you battled with your mother. If I could change what happened, then I would. I know that I should have taken you with me, I was a coward. But I'm not running anymore. I'm right here sweetheart. I'm right here……..'

Chapter Fifty.

22:34.

I look at the gun in my hand and shame engulfs me. The voice rages on, trying to gain my attention, but it doesn't work. It's hold over me has disappeared. My Dad's words stay with me. He's here, and he's going to look after me. A weird kind of calmness settles over me, and I allow myself to register the look of distress on Lacey's face.

"Oh my god, I'm so sorry Lacey," I say as I drop my hand holding the gun to my side and let tears fall from my eyes. My body shakes uncontrollably. Adrenaline pumps, but it no longer fuels my desire to hurt the woman in front of me.

"Put the gun down," I hear a strange voice behind me say sternly.

It's the police.

It's the fucking police.

You stupid cow. You couldn't just finish the job could you?

You couldn't just stick to the fucking plan. You had to let your dad's words play with your emotions. He's not actually here you know. He's a figment of your imagination.

I'm the one that has stood by you.

I'm the one that has looked out for you. And how do you repay me? By losing your nerve. By letting other people come between us.

I thought that you had seen sense.

I thought that we had reached a good place in our lives together.

But you disappoint me once again.

The voice is angry. The voice that has driven me mad for months. The voice that has always belonged to my mother, festering away in my brain.

"I'm sorry," I say out loud. "I'm sorry that I was never good enough for you, but it's time to put an end to it all now. I need to be free." The policeman behind asks me to put the gun down again and I look at it, my fingers wrapped around it.

"Kayleigh, please listen," Lacey pleads.

'I'm here sweetheart. I will make sure that you are okay.' My dad, reassuring me again. That's all I ever wanted. Reassurance and love.

It's time to make peace with myself.

It's time to lay the demons to rest.

This feels right.

This is how it was always supposed to end.

It's time to say goodbye to the pain.

Goodbye to the suffering.

Goodbye to the torment.

"Goodbye," I whisper as I close my eyes and move the gun so it is against my temple. Screams ring out all around me. Shouts from strangers fill my ears. Shrieks of alarm from all the bystanders.

It's funny how I can feel their terror and excitement all at once. How all of these people are looking at me and they are horrified but excited at the same time.

They will remember me as the woman with the gun.

The woman who could no longer go on.

The woman who took her own life in desperation.

As I get ready to pull the trigger, I smile because I know that I am actually the woman who set herself free...........

Chapter Fifty-One.

May 12th 2017.

I wake with a start, my eyes wide as I spring up to a sitting position in bed. I'm drenched with sweat, my heart is racing. Taking in deep lungful's of air, I try to calm myself down.

"You okay babe?" Ben says beside me as he pushes himself into a sitting position, his arm going around me. "Jesus Kayleigh, you're shaking like a leaf."

"Sorry, I just….. I had the most horrendous dream."

"Dream or nightmare?" Ben says as he pulls me against his chest. I nestle into him, relishing in his comforting embrace. We stay like that for a few moments as I wait for my heartbeat to return to normal. "Want to talk about it?" he asks, ever the doting fiancé.

"Not really."

"Okay. Well, I'll go and make us both a coffee." He places a kiss on the top of my head and releases me from his embrace. A cold chill runs over me as he gets out of bed and leaves the room. I freeze as I hear five words that tell me what the future holds.

Now you know the plan…………

THE END.

Author Acknowledgments.

I would like to say a big thank you to my other half James for his support, and to my family for continuing to encourage me. To my friends who have heard about Fixation for so long, I apologise for the wait but I hope that it has been worth it!

To my readers, thank you for taking the time to read my novels. I hope that you have enjoyed my psychological thriller as much as you enjoyed my romantic suspense books.

To Vikki, thank you for another awesome cover! I appreciate all of the time and effort that has gone into the design work, and it truly does look amazing.

And to my children, I love you both very much!

To keep up to date with my projects/book news, you can follow me on social media.
Facebook: www.facebook.com/lindseypowellperfect
Twitter: www.twitter.com/Lindsey_perfect
Instagram: www.instagram.com/lindseypowellperfect
Goodreads: www.goodreads.com/lpow21

I would be very grateful if you could leave me a review on amazon (and goodreads!)
Reviews are precious, even if they are only a few words.
Much love,
Lindsey.

28892053R00117

Printed in Poland
by Amazon Fulfillment
Poland Sp. z o.o., Wrocław